# Of Cats and Curiosity

## by

## Laura Strickland

*Mud, Debt and Gears*

**Of Cats and Curiosity**

Cover Art by *Tina Lynn Stout*

The Wild Rose Press, Inc.
PO Box 708
Adams Basin, NY 14410-0708
Visit us at www.thewildrosepress.com

Publishing History
First Edition, 2025
Trade Paperback ISBN 978-1-5092-6288-5
Digital ISBN 978-1-5092-6289-2

*Mud, Debt and Gears*
Published in the United States of America

## Dedication

For my friend and fellow author, Kim Turner,whose
gift to me inspired this series.

Chapter One

"Somethin' must be done about the Cats. Their abuse of power and their hold upon the City grow more extreme by the day. Each and every one of our woes might be laid at their—er—paws."

The meeting up under the eaves of the old wooden tavern had been in session no more than fifteen minutes before the outburst came. No great surprise to Livie, who stood over against the wall apart from the others gathered at the big, scarred table, listening. Someone always brought up the Cats. Usually, it took a little longer.

In this case the man who spoke, called Billy Spade because he kept a garden allotment in the cramped wasteland behind his house, had worked himself up into such a fervor that white foam gathered at the corners of his mouth. Had he been a member of the Dogs' League rather than a human, he'd be suspected of rabies.

Not that mechanical Dogs could get rabies.

Livie leaned against the rough boards behind her, the position chosen because it was near the door and offered potential escape, and eyed the motley group gathered around the table.

A rough-looking bunch, and no mistake, all under the age of forty—for the Great Killing had spared only the younger members of society, and few enough of those. All dressed in rags, all wet to the skin, for as usual it rained outside, the world continually weeping. All of

1

them angry.

"Of course all our woes can be laid at the paws of the Cats," a man called Sammy Bridle spat back into Billy's face. Not that Sammy married folk—he worked for the Horse League. Or should Livie say *slaved* for them?

Because when it came down to it, every human in the city of League was no better than a slave.

"They're the top of the heap," said Nellie, a woman of perhaps forty, whose wild mop of hair had already begun to turn gray. "And they're bleedin' us dry."

"Financially and morally," agreed Marty Coffin who worked in the graveyard and found himself something of a moral guide for them all. "I do not know which is worse."

"Not having bread to put on the table is worst," said a woman called Betty. "I have two children." She said the last proudly, it being the unspoken goal of every human left on the planet to put forth an effort and increase their population. Of course the children, being born, then needed to be fed. She had a tear in her eye. "Most nights they go to bed hungry."

"The Cats have no conscience," declared Bobby Trundle. "They don't care how much pain they cause us."

And Billy leaned toward the others to say, "They enjoy causin' us pain. They're Cats, ain't they? Didn't the *real* cats used to play with their prey before killin' it? These laws and…and rules they keep imposin' are just most sophisticated ways of playin' with us."

He might be right. Livie thought of the mechanical, steam-powered Cats who were in truth as closely related to ordinary felines as an educated man to an ape.

Not that there were educated men anymore. Just pitiful specimens such as these, bleating out their grievances at meetings in the hidden top rooms and basements of businesses.

Because God help them all if the authorities ever found out they did meet this way, it being strictly forbidden.

The Great Killing, which had occurred some thirty years ago, had eliminated most life on their planet. Indeed, some scholars said it was a way for the planet to rid itself of the inhabitants bent upon sucking it dry. If so, it had been an extraordinarily effective strategy.

Though the Killing had affected all forms of life, the deaths had been disproportionate. Humans had perished in the millions, with most the doctors gone. Only a small number survived.

An even larger proportion of animals had also died. It was said virtually none remained. But there had been someone here in League willing to preserve at least the *idea* of them.

They used to call him the Mechanic or the Great Mechanic, but now he was addressed by the sole name of Lord High. A human like them, he was also utterly unlike them, for he had not only survived the Killing but had thereafter turned on his fellow man.

Using his great knowledge of mechanics, he'd chosen to restore the animals. Improved and mechanized them. Left the humans to die or, at best, struggle at the bottom of the mud heap that had become their world. Set up a new order wherein people like Livie, and those gathered here with her, lived at the behest of the mechanicals he'd created.

Such disregard and indifference outreached even

that of the Cats, and argued that the Lord High must have detested his fellow man, back before all this began.

Sometimes, late at night, Livie thought about it. Back before the Great Killing, had the man been a hermit? A victim of some kind, in the world that had been before? A castoff perhaps, shunned or despised. Hard to believe there had been no other humans he'd cared—or still cared—to protect.

Instead, he'd turned to animals, mechanical ones, that was. He'd built them by the hundreds using the tools and components of the industrial age in which they'd once lived. He'd begun with the Cats and they now stood—on their back two legs—at the top of their society.

Few humans had ever seen the Lord High. Livie certainly hadn't. He had a grand workshop at the top of Castle Hill from whence he never, ever emerged, instead sending out his favored agents to accomplish his directives for him.

The laws the Cats imposed supposedly came from him, but Livie sometimes wondered.

"There must be a way to kill the Cats," said Betty wretchedly.

"How?" Marty challenged. "They're made of metal and fur. They have gears and cogs, and run on steam. They don't have hearts so we can't stab 'em. If we break off a limb, they'll just go to the Lord High for repairs. He takes care of them."

"And the consequences," Nellie breathed. "The punishment for harming one of his creatures is dire."

So it was. Terrible things had been done to humans who damaged any animal in the City. No matter to which League that animal belonged.

Beheadings. Maiming. At the very least, terrible imprisonments. Of those who had seen the Lord High, few lived to tell of it.

"Somethin' must be done," declared Denny Dustman, whose name was self-evident. "Why should we be at the bottom of the heap? We were at the top, in the old days."

"That was a long time ago," quavered Nellie, "before the world turned on its head."

"I know they're hard to kill," said Billy, "but we must be able to think of a way. They're just cats, when all's said and done. Big, dangerous cats. We must be able to outsmart them."

"Ye think ye're smarter than a Cat, do ye?" Marty asked. "They're devious, they are. Minds like steel traps."

A big man called Benny Lightman spoke for the first time. Though he attended most such meetings as this, Livie noted he rarely spoke up, just sat there like a living mountain. Of course, she usually attended and rarely spoke either. "A man created 'em. Created all the mechanical animals. A man should be able to take 'em down."

The pronouncement started a moment of silence, as if each human there contemplated that not-so-simple truth.

"But," Betty whispered then, "he's not just a human, is he? He's the Lord High."

Benny grunted. His job, granted to him on account of his height no doubt, was to ignite the steam lamps that illuminated the city. Since dark even now fell outside, he would need to leave the meeting soon.

But he said, "We've got to be clever, is all."

"Oh, is that all?" asked Danny Barman with sarcasm. He was a young man, used to surviving by his charm and his chatter behind the bar of a pub. "More clever than a Cat."

"What did the old tales say?" Someone spoke without warning. Livie realized, with surprise, it was her.

She, who never spoke out.

They all turned their heads and looked at her there by the door.

"Old tales?" repeated Sammy, as if it was an absurdity, which it was.

Livie barely remembered her parents. Her ma had died of overwork and starvation when Livie was six. Her dad, it was rumored, had perished in prison. But Ma had recited poems and little bits of wisdom to her, and those had gone deep.

She grunted. "Curiosity killed the cat."

Another dead silence met the words before Billy said, "That's an old one, that is."

"Curiosity," said Benny, "is an emotion. Do the League Cats experience emotions?"

She met his gaze, surprised he would ask a question so—well, intelligent. His eyes were mud brown, and he was frowning.

"Why not? Sure, they're mechanical. But they're still Cats deep inside. And they experience satisfaction, don't they, when they torment us?"

"S'pose so," he grunted.

"So how," asked Billy, "do we use their curiosity against them?"

"Don't know, really." Livie stirred beside the door. "Have to come up with somethin'—since we're so clever."

"All I know is," Marty took it up again, rampant with resentment, "we have to do somethin' before they bleed us all dry."

Livie sighed inwardly. It was the same every time. They complained and complained but nothing practical ever got done.

Benny Lightman rumbled a little as he got to his feet, his chair scraping back on the rough plank floor. "Gettin' dark. Have to start my rounds."

The rest of them took it as a signal.

"Next Monday?" Billy asked. "I'll let ye know the place."

Without waiting for assents or objections, Livie slipped out the door and down the rickety steps. The wet, foul air of the City embraced her.

Dark was, indeed, just falling, not but it had been gloomy with rain all day. In the City of League—indeed, the world over—it rained most all the time, an effect of whatever had happened to their climate during the Great Killing. One of the results of near constant precipitation, apart from the difficulties in growing food, was that mud prevailed. It coated every surface and stretched in broad swathes over every unimproved plot of land. It splashed boots and clothing and carriages and buildings.

The air reeked of it.

A very odd scent, had mud, one difficult to describe. Ripe and organic and cloying all at once. It got inside a woman's nostrils and refused to leave her brain alone.

There was no escaping it.

The pub that occupied the bottom floor of the building where they'd met was going strong, spilling light out through the open door and windows. Raised voices, curses, a snatch of song. People who had far too few choices in life came to such places to drown their sorrows. Livie could not imagine how they could afford it, with everyone in debt and not enough coin for food, let alone drink.

She started off along the street briskly, her head tucked down against the driving rain, wishing she could afford a cab, knowing she couldn't.

Someone fell into step beside her, skipping a bit to keep up with her long strides. Darting a look at her uninvited companion, she stifled a sigh. Danny Barman, at it again.

Danny, with his garrulous tongue and his well-practiced patter, considered himself a ladies' man.

He was not at all bad-looking with his mop of fair hair and his gap-toothed smile. But he was not what she was looking for—if, indeed, she was looking for anything, which she wasn't. And all he really wanted was to get under her skirts.

"Slow down, Livie," he said now. "I want to talk to ye."

"Can't." She tucked her head down tighter and walked faster. "Have to be at work at dawn." She cleaned four houses a day and daren't be late to any of them.

"Wait, wait." He seized her elbow and towed her to a halt. "There's more to life than workin'.."

"Is there?" If there was, Livie hadn't heard of it.

He leaned close. She could barely glimpse his face in the depths of his raised hood. "Sure."

"Aren't ye supposed to be behind the bar?" Danny had a place at the very tavern where they'd met. In fact he'd got them permission to meet there. She suggested, "Shouldn't ye go back?"

"I'm off tonight. D'ye want to make a child?"

"What?" That fairly nailed her feet to the wet pavement. The rain crashed down, soaking through the fabric of her coat, which was not of the right sort of keep her dry.

"Ye and me. We'll go back to your place, it's closer. Ye live on Becker Street, right?"

She drew her elbow from his grasp. "No."

"Ye don't live on Becker Street? I thought ye did."

"No, I don't want to make a child." With him. With anyone.

"But it's our duty. To make new life, increase our number. Ye know it is."

So the authorities—the human authorities that was, who had no real authority at all—preached to them. The animals that the Lord High had created and set in place could not reproduce. Only the human population, of whom so pitifully few remained, could increase its numbers.

Even then, not all females, so it had emerged, proved fertile. And of those who could bring squalling infants into the world, who could afford to raise them?

Danny leaned toward her again. "Don't ye want to do your duty?" he asked suggestively.

"Oh, a fine idea," she declared, anger beginning to burn through the affront. "And how am I supposed to do my work scrubbin' floors with a great bulge of a babe in my belly?"

The enthusiasm that lit his features, deep within the hood, died away. "Women are made for it, aren't they?"

Women who had someone to help look after them, perhaps. Not those forced to work as hard as Livie did.

She told him coolly, "Haven't ye done enough of your duty?" From what she'd heard of him, he'd seduced so many women his progeny—and potential progeny—must be spread clear across the City by now.

"One can never do enough of one's duty in that regard."

Livie snorted. "No, thanks."

"But—" he began, and caught hold of her elbow again.

Livie became dimly aware of footsteps coming behind them, barely audible over the clatter of the rain. She felt a large form looming up.

"Is there a problem here?"

Danny turned and let go of Livie's elbow.

"Oh, hello, Benny."

Ah, Livie thought. So it was. The Lightman must have followed them from the meeting, likely headed in their direction.

He edged his bulk forward, effectively bumping Danny away.

"No problem," Danny said. "I'm just seein' Livie home."

"Not a good idea to linger," Benny told him. "The Grey Guard will show up."

Livie shivered. The Grey Guard was made up from members of the Wolf League, and were to be avoided at all costs.

"In this rain?" Danny sounded mocking.

"They're out in all weathers. Miss Livie, perhaps ye would prefer me seein' ye home."

Perhaps she would. She could handle Danny, of course. But nothing about the big Lightman felt lascivious.

"Yes, please."

Danny gave a disgusted snort and took himself off,

swallowed almost immediately by the ever-increasing gloom.

Livie started walking again and Benny held the place at her side.

"I can take care of myself, ye know," she declared without looking at him.

"No doubt."

"And I would not want to make ye late for work. Shouldn't ye be on the job by now?"

"I have time enough to see ye safe home. Unless ye'd rather walk alone."

"No." Livie discovered somewhat to her surprise that she did not mind having the big man beside her. The mention of the Grey Guard made her uneasy. They patrolled in packs, and once they stopped you in the street, there was usually harassment.

She and her companion walked in silence for a few minutes, huddled against the rain, before Benny said, "I take it Danny put forward an unwanted suggestion."

"Yes." It annoyed Livie all over again. "I can't imagine why. I've never given him a bit of encouragement."

"I doubt his sort needs it. Though—" Benny stopped speaking abruptly and Livie slanted a look at him. Even though they'd attended many a meeting together, these were the most words she'd ever exchanged with the Lightman.

"Though?" she encouraged.

"I shouldn't say. Ye'll likely take it the wrong way and ye'll think as poorly of me as ye do of him."

That startled Livie to the point that she stopped walking. "Does it matter what I think of ye?"

"To me, it does."

He took her arm and it felt nothing like when Danny had grabbed her. "Best keep movin'. If the Grey Guard do spot us, they won't make a fuss so long as they think we're goin' some place."

"It's not much farther."

"Becker Street?"

"Yes. Benny, what were ye goin' to say?"

"Benton. Call me Benton. Givin' us diminutive names is a means the Cats use to diminish us. Steal our self-respect. Make us less. My parents named me Benton."

"All right." Did they have any self-respect?

"And that's the reason I don't think I should say what I would, to ye. I do not want to diminish ye in any way, maybe by reducin' ye to your appearance since ye're clearly so much more—"

"Just say it."

"Ye're so pretty. That's why he wants to be with ye."

They had reached Livie's door. She stepped up on the stone stoop, which still didn't make her as tall as Benton, and faced him.

She was not pretty. The assertion did not offend her in the way he might have thought, but only in so much as it was not true. She was too tall, and her hair was mouse brown. Her features were not delicate, her lips not sweetly bowed, her cheeks not rounded. She carried none of the hallmarks of beauty.

Why should this man stand here and lie to her? Unless—he too wanted to get under her skirt. Beggars could not be choosers.

"No," she said with a toss of her head, "I reckon he's just horny."

That startled a laugh from Benton. "Well, so long as ye can see it clearly, who's lyin' to ye and who's not. I don't lie, Miss Olivia."

Olivia. No one ever called her that. And yes, it did lend her a bit of pride. A fine name, and one with dignity.

"This is my house. Thanks for seein' me home."

He nodded and hurried off, head tucked down against the rain. Livie fumbled for the latch at the door, but before she could manage it, a harsh voice sounded behind her.

She spun. She could just see Benton's large figure disappearing down the street through the rain. Directly behind her, though, stood a Police Dog. The officer was tall, oversized for what would have been an actual dog, which it was not. This mechanical specimen, clearly meant to be an Alsatian, wore a blue uniform, highly-polished boots now well splashed with mud, and a suspicious gleam in its amber-brown eyes. Though it had the typical countenance of a dog, it had been skillfully altered and ran on a mechanism very similar to clockwork, though powered by steam.

Indeed, the interior lights, coming from behind Livie, caught a waft of vapor rising as the mechanical police officer spoke.

"You will tell me, Human, what you are doing out so late."

Livie's heart sank. One of the many rules governing humans' lives was the one saying that on work days, they were permitted out only to go to and from their jobs, or to purchase necessities. Most times that rule was not strictly enforced. People went to pubs, to visit one another, even to walk in the park—or to attend meetings of the ersatz resistance.

Just Livie's luck that she would meet up with a hard-nosed—or rather hard-snouted—member of the force tonight.

She glanced around for the Alsatian's partner. Police Dogs almost always traveled in pairs.

"I'm just arrivin' home from work, Officer."

"You live here?"

"Yes."

"Where do you work?"

"As a scrubwoman."

The Police Dog processed that. His intelligence was mechanical and could almost be observed to operate. His voice, when he spoke again, came in an odd growl. Something wrong with his voice box, perhaps, that needed repair.

"You should not be returning home this late from scrubbing."

"I—um—stopped for a drink. At the tavern."

"Arriving here late may cause a disturbance. You should behave in a respectful fashion."

"I did not mean to cause a disturbance, sir."

"Go inside and stay there until you report for your next shift."

"Yes, sir." Livie paid lip service, but a flare of anger took light inside her the way one of Benton's lamps might.

She did not need to be cowed by the Cats or intimidated by the Wolves or, indeed, ordered around by the Dogs. She was a human, by God.

And she'd be damned if she'd quit the fight for a better place in her world.

Chapter Two

It seemed to Livie that all she ever did was mop up mud. An inevitable part of life, so she supposed, given it rained damned near every day in her world, and she cleaned four homes a day, the same ones two days a week, and eight others on alternating days.

Mechanicals, no matter their League, were fussy about their houses and liked them kept clean. That did not mean they gave any regard to those who performed the cleaning. They would walk in over a spotless floor shedding the inevitable mud and rainwater as if they did not notice. They certainly did not notice the lowly woman who mopped up in their wake.

She honestly thought that, to her employers, she remained mostly invisible. That was likely why the Cats, or the Lord High, had created the League of House Mice to act as go-betweens and deal with the tiresome humans.

As a consequence of arriving home dead tired, the floors of her rooming house, occupied mostly by other scrubwomen like herself, rarely got cleaned at all. The house, not prepossessing in the first place—rooming houses for humans rarely were—became what could only be termed depressingly squalid.

Letting herself inside after the Police Dog finished with her, it struck her as worse than ever, and the anger that had ignited in her breast flared still hotter.

Indeed, the best thing that could be said for this

particular rooming house was that it was conveniently located adjacent to the neighborhoods of her betters so she might conveniently serve those betters. All the households Livie cleaned—twelve of them in total—were located near Becker Street. She walked everywhere.

But that meant her betters—the mechanicals—did not like to see her cluttering up their streets. Hence the warning from the Police Dog.

As she trudged wearily up the hollow stairs to her third-floor room, Livie contemplated her life, a vicious round. On Mondays and Thursdays, she cleaned the same four households. On Tuesdays and Fridays, another four, and a further four on Wednesdays and Saturdays. Sundays were her own. In return for all that labor, she earned a pittance. Not nearly enough to keep her solvent.

The shops and warehouses were all City owned, and humans paid dearly for everything they required to live. Food, clothing, the most basic of household goods. They paid rent for their humble rooms. Since there was never enough coin to go around, and the Cats were willing to hold notes, every human in the City lived in debt.

Debt so deep there was no hope of getting out. People just worked and strove and did as they must.

For her part, Livie did her best not to think about it. She'd started working to keep herself at the age of ten, and by twelve had been so deep in debt she had no hope of seeing daylight.

There wasn't a lot of daylight in League City.

Livie's room was small and poor, no more than ten paces by ten. And for this she worked nearly all the hours God sent. The house itself had once been fine, back in the old days, but it had been partitioned into tiny spaces with plank walls that meant she could hear her neighbors on either side, and she had no window, that having fallen to someone more fortunate.

Sleeping here was like lying in a wooden box. A coffin, perhaps. But better than having no roof at all, being out on the streets like some poor folk, forced to lie in the rain or under bridges. Constantly harassed, and sometimes brutalized, by the Dogs and Wolves.

She would do near anything to keep a roof—however poor—over her head.

She stripped off her wet clothing beginning with her coat, which she hung on the back of the door, and then everything else down to the skin. The garments would dry stiff, their most frequent washing by rain. She donned her nightgown but did so slowly, thinking about—

Thinking about Benny Lightman. *Benton.*

She had found, for the most part, it was best to think as little as possible. But the heat of her anger was dying, and she reached instinctively for something to keep her warm.

Did he admire her? Did he, truly?

She placed little stock in what men said. For the most part they ignored her because, as she'd told Benny, she was not pretty. Sometimes they might follow her with their eyes, for she was tall and female. But something off-putting about her usually made them look away again.

Only persistent rogues like Danny dared.

But Benny, now—Benton—what did she know about him? Precious little. He had attended most their meetings, sitting like a big, usually damp hillock, but he never said much. She knew he was a Lightman because they had all shared their jobs while discussing their plights.

Lighting lamps did not seem too bad, on the face of it. True, the light stands were high—she had seen the men shimmying up them with their flints. And yes, sometimes a lamp did explode from built-up gasses, with dreadful effects to the lighters. But it did not seem so demoralizing as the endless scrubbing.

However, such men were out in the rain—in the dark—all night, every night, available to whoever wanted to prey on them. A group of drunken Foxes returning from their club. Squads of Raccoons out thieving. Even bored members of the Grey Guard who wanted targets for their insidious aggression.

There had been some terrible stories. Stories of injuries, deaths.

So no, she did not envy Benny his position. Though—he was big enough to protect himself from all but the Wolves. Raising a hand against them meant dire consequences indeed, and yes, quite likely death.

She did not know much else about Benny. Except that against all likelihood he thought her *pretty*.

She did not possess a mirror but had seen herself often enough in those at the grand homes she cleaned. She could not imagine what he saw.

Yet he'd said it so matter-of-factly, without a hint of flattery, as if of course she was pretty.

And, she challenged herself as she settled into her narrow cot, was Benny what she would deem handsome?

No.

Few men she'd ever seen in the City could be deemed so, though men like Danny did achieve the status of good-looking.

Sadly, Benny did not warrant even that. Not that she supposed she'd ever got what might be called a decent look at him. He always attended meetings swathed in a huge, tan coat, often leaving the hood up, or with a hat well pulled down over his hair.

Almost as if he did not want people to see him.

She had glimpsed his eyes, which were mud brown. Not a very prepossessing color, and one that dominated their world, but they were fairly nice eyes, for all that. Large and well set under level brows. The brows dark brown, so his hair must be that shade also.

Other than that, she had only an impression of a broad face, stark with bone, and a generous mouth.

Was she interested in him?

No, God, no. She did not need those complications in her life.

What she needed was sleep. The morning would come very early and no excuses for being late to her work.

\*\*\*\*

"What if the Lord High were to die? What if somebody took him out? What would happen to us then?"

The query—or was it a plea?—came from one among the group of Lightmen gathered on the streetcorner. The fellows on Benton's route had taken to meeting for a quick pass of the flask on a corner halfway through the night. The cold tended to work right through to a man's bones by that point, and time stretched impossibly long till dawn.

No one had ever suggested, though, they should talk of sedition. Such words, if overheard, would bring execution of not only the speaker but all who listened to him.

Benton jerked his head around to locate the man who'd uttered the dangerous words, a wizened little fellow named Georgie, well past the average age. He must have survived the Great Killing, but would not last long if he kept flapping his lips in such a manner.

"Careful," he said. "Careful what ye say."

"Nobody here but us," Georgie replied.

"There are ears everywhere."

"And traitors?" asked Andy with a lifted brow. "Who's talkin' to the Cats?"

Andy was Benton's friend, if he could be said to have any. They'd been working adjacent routes a long time and sometimes met in the tavern after a shift. In fact, Andy was the one who'd first got Benton attending meetings of the resistance.

He liked Andy's sharp sense of humor that disguised his anger and hopelessness. Andy had married and possessed a family, which just made his lot that much harder, as far as Benton could see.

"No traitors here," declared Georgie, and Benton and Andy exchanged a look.

You never could tell. Men had been dragged off before for what the Cats called heresy.

But there was a feeling growing in the City, among its human population. More and more, at any gathering, talk turned to rebellion—ways and means. It was why Benton attended the regular meetings. He figured it safer than talking out here on the street.

And a man couldn't give up, could he? Couldn't just roll over beneath the Cats' claws?

"But what would happen?" Georgie persisted, lowering his voice. "If, say, someone got into the palace where he hides, and—"

"Impossible," said another fellow, Petie. "The man's a recluse livin' behind all kinds of protective walls. Hell, none of us has ever seen him. At least I haven't." He looked around, his sharp-featured, over-thin face making him appear hungry. "Have ye? Have ye?"

He was met with grunts, nothing more.

Another, smaller man across the circle from Benton said, "Whoever made the attempt would have to be willin' to sacrifice his life. Go into it knowin' he'd never get away."

"Assassination," breathed someone else in a spectral tone, and a shiver not caused by the cold wind chased its way up Benton's spine.

"All I asked," said the original speaker, "was what if he died? What would happen to us? How would it change our world?"

"The Cats would take over," a man called Mikey replied promptly.

"But they report to him."

"Yes, but can ye imagine them givin' up all that power they hold? Never happen."

"They might be worse than him, come to think on it."

"Nothin' could be worse than him."

The whispers came thick and fast now, fomented ideas pouring out. They'd been thinking on this, if too fearful to express those thoughts.

"Eventually the Cats—all of them—would fall into disrepair," said someone else—Benton was shocked to discover it was him. "Without him there to maintain 'em."

A brief silence fell as everyone took this in.

"Ye think so?" asked someone. "Some o' 'em can fix themselves."

"Small repairs, yes. Not all—"

"What is the meaning of this?" The query came from beyond their circle and sounded in a gravely growl that caused an instant spear of alarm. Authority lay in that growl, and inestimable threat.

The Grey Guard.

The ring of Lightmen broke apart and opened up to face the two figures that approached in tandem.

They often patrolled in numbers, did the guard, or *packs*, if you wanted to be precise about it. Usually, as now, they appeared in pairs, but you could bet if trouble broke out additional members would materialize. It was said they communicated by instinct, the raw, complicated instinct of wolves enhanced by the improvements the Lord High had given them.

This pair looked huge looming out of the dark. In truth, both were tall—at least as tall as Benton—and impressive in their official, long gray cloaks.

Like all of the Lord High's creations, they stood upright on their rear paws, those appendages being encased in faux leather boots. Each had visible repairs or augmentations—a rigged, furless metal front paw here, a bare ear there.

Their fur, thick and luxurious, gleamed where not covered by those grand cloaks, and their eyes—yellow eyes as feral as if they'd just come from the depths of some stygian forest—shone. They held their long muzzles open to show sharp, metal canines.

A thought—the repetition of a line from an ancient story appeared in Benton's head. *Grandmother, what large teeth you have*. But he felt nothing of levity.

The Grey Guard had always affected him profoundly. He did not like admitting that, but it was so. A visceral, primitive fear crawled up through him.

"Who gave you permission to gather here?" asked the Wolf on the right, he with the metal paw. The Lord High had done a wonderful job in giving his creatures voice. They sounded like what they were, and this came out in the kind of growl that made a man's blood run cold.

"Are you not supposed to be working?" asked his companion. "Lightmen."

The distress blooming around the circle was palpable. It might be one thing to speak sedition while alone. In the face of the Guard, all such defiance flew.

"We are workin', sir," said Georgie.

The first Wolf focused on him. A new sharpness— that of the predator—appeared in his eyes. "It does not appear so."

"Just takin' a wee break," said another man congenially. One did not—absolutely did not—want to draw the Wolf's attention.

How much had they heard before they stepped up? They moved so quietly they might have been there in the dark a while, listening before they approached. Their hearing was extraordinary, and one of them had that enhanced ear.

Had they heard what he said?

As if in answer, the first Wolf flicked a glance at him, one that froze him where he stood.

"The lamps are all lit, Master," said Mikey respectfully. "We got 'em all lit."

"And are you not then supposed to continue your

23

Laura Strickland

rounds making certain they stay lit in the wet till dawn, and then extinguish them again?"

"Yes, sir."

"Then why are you standing here? Go back to work."

Benton felt painful relief. This could have gone two ways. The whole lot of Lightmen—or certain ones among them, serving as examples—might have been hauled away. Or they might have been given a warning. It looked like they'd got off easy.

"Wait," said the second Wolf. His ear, the one that was not mechanical, flicked forward. "Of what were you talking?"

If possible, Benton's heart plummeted still more violently. The Wolf had heard them after all.

"Just talkin' of our families, and such like," said Georgie bravely.

The Wolves conferred in that disquieting way they had, inclining their heads to one another, not speaking a word.

The first Wolf said to Georgie, "You will come with us."

"No," said Georgie instantly. "My route. My route—"

"Another will finish your route. And—" the Guard's sharp, yellow gaze moved around the circle, touched on Benton for an endless moment, and moved on again to Petie. "You."

"What have I done? Sir?"

"Come. You others cover their routes until new assignments can be made."

*New assignments.* That meant those being arrested could not expect to come back.

24

"The rest of you, back to work." The words came in a terrifying snarl that scattered the men.

Other Wolves appeared out of the dark and took Georgie and Petie into custody. Georgie was still protesting as they moved down the street.

Benton's gaze met Andy's. "They'll question 'em," Andy breathed. "Question 'em."

Yes indeed. Not mere questions and answers, though it might start out that way. There would be claws, metal claws involved. Pain and blood.

"They'll tell everythin'. The rest of us are lost."

Benton swore under his breath. But he moved off as he did, back toward his route. Through the pounding rain and back into servitude.

Because there was always something worse. Worse than the wet and the drudgery. The hopelessness. The cowardice.

Georgie and Petie were about to experience that *worse*.

So even though he cursed his own lack of balls as he went, Benton did go. For he knew how close he'd come to it being him.

When the Wolf's gaze had touched on him, he'd been certain he would be dragged away. That he'd been overheard. He'd felt what it was to be prey.

Could he withstand the questioning? No, of course not. No one could. A man only deceived himself if he supposed so.

Why had the Wolf let him go? They were intelligent creatures—the top of the Lord High's hierarchy—and he'd given them lightning-fast thinking capacity. There would be a reason.

He did not like it, whatever it was. Perhaps he would

be followed. Watched. Eyes could be on him even now.

It did not have to be the Wolves themselves. The Grey Guard had many agents. The Dogs served as guards and peacekeepers. The Coyotes were everywhere, if but rarely seen, and the Ferrets could slip through the shadows and, it was said, cracks but half their size. The Raccoons were born thieves and could get in anywhere, and as for the Foxes—

Well, they were too clever and tricky for mere men to outsmart.

It was said that after the Great Killing, the Lord High had saved and enhanced the animal residents of the world as retaliation for what such creatures had suffered over the centuries at the hands of men. The fox hunts, the deer hunts, the mouse traps, the shooting competitions, the casual cruelty and near-extermination. He'd preferred—by far—animals to men and had chosen to level the playing field.

He'd done more than level it, though. He'd tilted it so far in the animals' favor that mankind, already in severe minority, did not stand a chance.

Yes, Benton had heard the tales of past cruelties. Cows imprisoned in barns by the thousands, never seeing the green of a field, for the sake of their milk, their offspring taken from them at birth. Now bovines oversaw all farming that got done in the wet climate— and humans paid dearly for what they grew.

Just as Deer and Boars were now the guardians of the woodlands, and anyone who attempted to hunt there, be it only to feed his family, faced a swift and merciless fate.

The Lord High had instituted his own idea of justice. He was clever enough—and powerful enough—to enforce it.

Back on his route, Benton saw that one of his lamps had gone out. He sighed and shimmied up the pole to relight it. This, until dawn, at which time he would have to go back and extinguish them all.

Such was his life. Lighting fires for a brief time only to put them out again. A pointless existence. But now—

Now fear hovered in the back of his mind. The Wolf had looked at him.

What would happen if the Lord High died? Would the structure of this world he had built collapse? Would men then be able to find a more just position for themselves?

The Lord High could not live forever. Could he?

Not unless he'd found a way to enhance himself as he had the animals he favored. Perhaps the Lord High was no longer completely human.

That thought terrified Benton so much he thrust it to the back of his mind and thought only about his work for the rest of the night.

Chapter Three

"You will do a particularly careful job of cleaning the sitting room," Mistress Mariel Tom instructed Livie. "We are expecting guests tonight."

"Yes, Mistress Tom," Livie answered by rote.

Mistress Mariel's house was the first of her assignments that day, a grand stone dwelling which must once have belonged to wealthy humans. All the finest houses in the City had been given to members of the Cat League, though some of the Grey Guard possessed nearly as much wealth. They—the Wolves—preferred a slightly different lifestyle.

Livie cleaned only one Wolf dwelling, on Wednesdays and Saturdays. The place terrified her almost as much as its occupants.

Mistress Mariel gave Livie a severe glare. She was a beautiful Cat, as were so many members of her League, long-haired and elegant with golden gears visible at her throat and a blue jewel set into her forehead. Her eyes were also blue, her fur a mixture of gray and white that flowed beneath her clothing. Elegant, she was, and deceptively sweet of expression.

One did not want to displease her.

Livie had the scars to prove it.

Her husband worked in the higher echelons of the government, and Livie rarely saw him. He was a ginger tom, much larger than his dainty wife, with an air of self-important preoccupation. He wore frock coats and a monocle.

"As for the foyer," continued Mistress Mariel, gesturing to the grand entryway, "I do not want to see a speck of mud."

An impossible demand. Mud was endemic in their world. The streets outside ran and splashed with it. Livie had herself brought some in on her boots.

"And the front steps," Mistress Mariel added.

Livie groaned inwardly though of course she did not let the Cat hear.

"I will be sending Mistress Yarrow to report."

Mistress Yarrow was the head House Mouse, the equivalent of a housekeeper. And she had no hesitation in squeaking off to Mariel if she saw something she did not like.

Livie had only three hours to get everything perfect. It was now six a.m. She needed to be at her second assignment by nine, the third at noon, the last at three. After six, if she did not run over, her time would be her own.

She had a feeling she would run over today.

She started with the foyer and moved on to the parlor, leaving the other rooms for little more than a quick tidying. Today was Monday and she had not been here since last Thursday—the mud traces were considerable. While the House Mice might tidy the rooms on other days, they did not scrub, considering it beneath them.

That was Livie's twelve-hour day.

Clocks ruled any mechanical's home. Some said it was because, before the Great Killing, the Lord High had been a clockmaker. Livie didn't know, but the case clock in the hallway had chimed eight forty-five when a delivery of flowers arrived. The House Mice instructed the delivery Horses to distribute the displays in both foyer and sitting room, resulting in wide-spread muddy boot prints.

Livie sighed and got down on her hands and knees again. She would be late to her second assignment. She would run late all day.

She did not arrive at her second assignment till nine-thirty, and the head House Mouse there greeted her with what passed for a scowl. The home belonged to a pair of wealthy Raccoons who were sleeping, as it happened. Sometimes the Bandits were astir when Livie arrived and she could tidy their bedroom. But not today.

They must have had a late night of thieving.

Among members of the Racoon League, thieving was considered a talent and in fact was approved, a matter of pride. The more opulent a Raccoon's home, the more proficient he was seen to be at his vocation.

This pair must indeed be proficient, for the house was lavish if gaudy. Many of their possessions might well have been stolen from others and made an eclectic assortment. Unlike the Cats, they were untidy, leaving belongings strewn about in a careless fashion.

Livie began with scrubbing muddy footprints and moved on to tidying. When she left at twelve-fifteen, the Raccoons were still sleeping—if indeed mechanicals truly needed to sleep, and did not just ape the habits of their more authentic ancestors.

She usually tried to grab a bite to eat between her morning and afternoon shifts. No time for that today, even though her stomach rumbled.

Her third home on Mondays and Thursdays

belonged to a Wolf. She dared not be any later than she could help.

The house was an austere one, tall and narrow with a gabled roof. Built of stone, it was usually scrupulously neat inside. All rooms but one, for in the course of her duties, Livie had seen the bedroom and it was—well, as different from the rest of the house as could be. Kept dark with heavily-draped windows, it was all bed, a monstrously-sized structure piled with furs. It reminded Livie of nothing so much as a den.

Perhaps it was. Possibly even mechanical Wolves answered to that instinct and the resident—a member of the infamous Grey Guard—spent all her time here when at home. For the rest of the house definitely felt unused.

That should have made Livie's job easier, but a trail of the relentless mud led from the front door up the stairs to the bedroom and household members such as the House Mice had muddied the kitchen.

Livie got to work.

She had become fairly adept at cleaning up mud, as much so as anyone could be, for it was an insidious substance neither liquid or solid that, rather than allowing itself to be mopped away, just smeared. It had a firm grip on their world, emerging from the very cobbles of the streets and stones of the walls, the grass verges and edges of yards, merging with the rain and spreading. It had a smell all its own, that stank of the river which ran through the middle of League, with a bright overlay of animal. It got up Livie's nose, and every day she went home stinking of it.

One good thing about cleaning the home of the Grey Guard was that apart from the House mouse who admitted Livie—in this case an individual reminiscent of a diminutive butler who rarely spoke—she usually saw no one. Her employer tended to be out at work, perhaps at the Guard headquarters or on patrol somewhere in the City.

Not so, today. Livie was scrubbing mud off the wall in the little corridor that led to the back hall when a prickling began in her spine. Though she'd heard absolutely nothing, she could feel someone there.

She turned and froze.

Just because her employer was female—according to how the House Mouse spoke of her, for who could tell?—did not make her small. She loomed over Livie, being some six feet in height, perfectly motionless there at the end of the hallway.

She was not dressed in her uniform of metallic armor covered by a gray cloak. Was it her day off? Did mechanicals require days off? Instead she wore a fine, patterned robe of jewel colors, open at the neck to display—

Well, her mechanics, Livie supposed those were. A cluster of moving gears and pistons, well-surrounded by luxurious fur, all powered by the small coal fire that burned at the heart of all mechanicals.

Her long muzzle, gray frosted with white, was closed, emitting no trace of steam. Her ears were pricked, high and attentive. Her eyes—

Oh, by God, her eyes. They were golden, cold, calculating, and merciless. Fixed upon Livie as if she saw nothing else.

Livie froze. It was an instinct far older than the existence of League or any occupation, as old as humankind itself. That of prey caught in the gaze of the predator, for that was how the Guard looked at her.

*She will not kill me*, Livie told herself with desperate persuasion. *She will not eat me. Why should she? They do not eat food.*

But the way the Guard regarded Livie argued she might kill her just for the pleasure of it. Death would be swift, violent, and bloody. This was no Cat, after all.

Livie wondered a bit madly who would clean the blood off the walls after she was dead.

She pressed her back to the damp wall. "Good day, Mistress Wolf. Am I in your way?" She spoke in an effort to break that somehow holy connection between predator and prey, to abolish that terrifying look in the golden eyes.

One leap. The silent Wolf stood near enough that it would take no more.

The Wolf parted her jaws to speak. Her voice came out in a growl that was somehow also silky. Each mechanical built by the Lord High had its own voice box, and its own custom-built intelligence.

"Were you late today?"

"Yes, Mistress, I was. My first assignment of the mornin' was havin' a house party. There was extra work to be done." Livie despised herself for answering so meekly. Yet despite the severe confines of her existence, she suddenly discovered she wanted very much to stay alive. And her fear still had a hold on her.

The Wolf made a curious tutting sound that showed her teeth.

"I do not like excuses."

"No, Mistress."

"You are expected to be on time."

"Yes, Mistress. I could not help it."

"Is your first client so much more important than

me, that you should put his or her needs ahead of mine?"

"No indeed, Mistress."

"It will not happen again."

"It will not."

"Because if it does, do you know what I will do to you?"

Livie shook her head, still held by that stare which had not wavered, unable to speak.

The Wolf leaned closer. "I shall rend you limb from limb. No more excuses, understand?"

Livie nodded. The Wolf released her at last from the potent stare and glanced around the hallway as if seeking more fault to find. Apparently finding none, she moved off as suddenly as she had come.

Livie scrambled to her feet and stood for several moments while the rush of fear subsided and her thundering heartbeat calmed.

They did that kind of thing because they could. Because at the heart of all the mechanics, they were still animals. Cats or Dogs or Ferrets or Wolves.

Cats were frightening. They were capricious and could report a human on a whim, have you turned over to authorities. Imprisoned.

Nothing could be more terrifying than a conviction of imminent death.

She finished her work as swiftly as she could and departed the house, back out into the rain, telling herself, *I don't have to come back here till Thursday and by then the Wolf will likely be out at work.*

But as she moved on to her final assignment of the day, she could not help but think how unfair it all was.

Once all these houses had belonged to humans, back when League had been a city by another name. Families had lived there in comfort. Now humans—by far a minority—were allowed into them only as servants.

In the old days, so she imagined, mice were kept out at any cost. Now the dwellings were turned over to them for their keeping just as Racoons—once shot and trapped as pests—were at leave to steal. Foxes were at leave to play the lord at gaming dens. Dogs, serving as policemen, now assured that humans would be obedient.

In the injustice there lay a certain justice—Livie could see that—as well as irony. She wondered about the Lord High, who had orchestrated it all.

Was he a man who prized irony?

She herself did not appreciate it, at least not when it was aimed at her personally.

By the time she finished cleaning her fourth house of the day, which belonged to a Hare trained as an Herbalist, fortunately not at home, her hands were raw and her back ached. Beneath the curtain of rain she trudged her way home, only to be lured by the bright lights of a tavern.

Not the one where Danny Barman worked, but another from whence she could hear music and—much more alluring—laughter. She shouldn't go in, merely because she could not afford to drink. If she wasted money here, she would not have enough for her rent. Not that she'd get tossed out of her lodgings. That rarely happened. But a black mark would go in the Overseer House Mouse's book and she would slide just that much farther into debt.

Yet—there would be food inside. She had eaten what should have been her lunch late, and it had made a poor dinner.

She deserved a bite to eat, didn't she? And a few

minutes within that light, following her long, dismal day.

She went in. She'd never before entered this particular tavern, though she'd passed it often. Now the warmth and humanness of it embraced her. Did humans need to be among other humans?

They were kept so often isolated.

It was said that, were one arrested by the Dogs or, God forbid, the far more terrifying Grey Guard, one of the cruelest punishments was to be shut in a small stone cell completely alone. Just left there with very little food, light, or distractions of any kind for days uncounted.

They said sometimes that broke a man even when torture couldn't.

But here were faces and voices and—yes—bright hints of laughter. As she made her way to the bar, she wondered whether she might have been precipitous in sending Danny away so summarily. No, she did not want to carry or birth a child, or to raise one, something quite impossible in her situation. But the being with someone—even if it was the mildly repugnant Danny— and intimate with him—as surely breeding would require—might just be worth it.

The barman here was squat and quite ugly. He gave Livie an assessing look as she leaned on the bar.

"Bad day, chickie?"

"They're all bad. But yes, this was worse than most."

"What can I get ye?"

If she had a drink, she would fall flat on her back within minutes. "What do ye have to eat?"

"Soy bites. Baked potatoes. Grilled aubergine."

"Let me have a potato." Since the Great Killing, eating meat was strictly forbidden.

"All the fixin's?" The barman grinned at her.

"Yes, please."

As she waited for her potato, she surveyed the room. The place was not large, but it was crowded, which made her hope the food would be good.

Since mechanicals did not need to eat, foodstuffs, like everything else in their world, were strictly controlled. Given the altered climate, most food could only be grown in greenhouses, though some herbs, flowers, rice and potatoes still struggled to grow out in the mud fields. Grown only for human consumption, release of food was restricted. Never quite enough. Some people did have allotments, but not much grew there.

"So," said the barman while they waited for her potato, making her turn back to him, "what was so bad about your day?"

"Ye wouldn't believe it."

"I would. Ye should hear what I listen to on a daily basis. Best to get it out, lassie."

"It's just so unfair. All of it." To Livie's horror, she choked up. Could she be so weak as to cry in front of this stranger?

But that was the point, wasn't it? He was a stranger and yet he was a fellow human, so again he was not a stranger. He felt her pain. He felt, full stop, in a way that the beings she encountered all day didn't.

Perhaps that was, indeed, why Danny was bent on impregnating the city.

Her potato arrived, reasonably large and smothered in fake cream and faux bacon. She took it and began looking for a place to sit.

That was when she saw him. The truth was, he was too big to miss for long, even though he'd squashed himself into a seat in the corner and sat looking at no one.

She made her way to him, walking carefully.

"Hello, Benton. Mind if I share your table?"

He looked up in surprise. He had a newssheet—one of the outdated ones—on the table in front of him and had been surreptitiously reading it.

He half got to his feet, making the table heave. "Olivia. Please do."

There was barely room. She put down her potato and squeezed in opposite him.

He had pushed the hood of his sopping cloak back on his shoulders, so she got a good look at him in the smoky light. That wide face, so strong in the cheekbones. The steady, mud-colored gaze. Livie supposed she should classify his eyes as brown, but to be sure, she saw mud everywhere she looked.

His hair was much darker, as were his level brows and the scruff that grew along his jaw.

His hands, resting on the table, were large and bore burn scars. A lot of them.

For some reason, regarding him so sent a little thrill through her, so rare and odd she failed to recognize it for what it was.

"Rough day?" he asked.

Was it visible on her? She supposed so.

"Yes. Yes, it was." Suddenly she wanted to tell him about it, to spill out all the details of her woes. To have him sit quietly and listen.

Instead, she dug into her potato. "Don't think me rude but I'm starvin'."

"Enjoy it," he bade, and tried not to watch her eat.

He had dark lashes—unexpectedly long—and as dark as his hair, wet with the rain. Livie wondered abruptly what his body looked like, and caught that thrill again.

He had a half full glass of ale in front of him and when she'd eaten most of her potato, he pushed it toward her.

"Have some."

"Ye don't mind?"

He shook his head and she drank, trying not to be greedy. The ale tasted slightly sour. Home brew, like most taverns served.

"Thank ye," she said, setting the glass back down and shoving it toward him.

"Finish it, if ye like. I rarely drink. It's an excuse to sit here in the warm more than anythin' else."

She lifted her gaze to him. Big. Immovable. Somehow trustworthy. "Ye start your shift soon?"

"Soon. I have a few minutes. Want to talk about it?"

The same offer the barman had made, more or less. But this did not seem so much like mere lip service.

So she told him, letting it all spill out after all, from the seas of inescapable mud to the fright given her by the Grey Guard. By the time she finished her potato was gone and so was the last of his ale.

"It's just so unfair," she cried. "Look at my hands. Look at them." She thrust them out across the table, regarding them with a kind of horror. They were red and raw, cracked along the sides of the fingers, visibly sore. Again, she felt tears clog her throat.

Benton might have done many things. Expressed sympathy, murmured words, tried to reason out her plight. Instead, he took her abused hands in his, enfolded them gently and tenderly.

His hands were so much larger than hers and so

careful despite their scars, that she felt—well, she supposed *protected* made an apt word. Maybe even *cherished*.

His eyes filled with compassion. He said only, "It's hard."

"And unfair," she bleated again.

"And unfair."

"I was so—so frightened of the Wolf. She frightened me on purpose. What right does she have to do that?"

Benton shrugged. "We are at the bottom of the food chain. The lowest of the low. They think of us as muck dwellers who writhe and reproduce—all beneath them."

"There's a sort of justice in that," she voiced her earlier thoughts, "given the way mankind treated animals in the past. But there's no personal justice. For me." He still held her hands, and she discovered she didn't particularly want him to let go.

He told her, speaking softly and calmly, about his experience the night before with the Grey Guard patrol.

"I understand why ye were frightened," he said, his thumbs now very gently caressing the raw skin on her hands. It felt like a balm. "Those primitive feelin's just rise."

"What do ye think will happen to those men who were taken? Petie and Georgie."

"George and Peter," he corrected. "They give us those diminutive names to make us seem less."

"Yes." She managed a smile. "Benton."

"Olivia." Very carefully, he folded her hands together and gave them back to her. "I'm afraid I need to go to work."

"Yes." She felt a pang. "Do ye hate your job?"

"No. Except it's out in the wet." He gave a

surprisingly mischievous smile. "And there's always a chance of fallin' from a slippery lamp pole. At least it's outdoors—in the wet."

"Ah, yes. Benton, thank ye for—" she gestured at his empty glass, "for this."

"It's nothin'."

It wasn't nothing. He just might have saved some vital part of her.

He got to his feet, causing an earthquake for the table.

Livie rose too and did something she never did. "Can I see ye again?" She asked and blushed fiercely. "That is, can we meet like this again?" She never, ever reached for men. That way lay ruination.

He gave her another long look from those mud-colored eyes.

"I daresay we'll see each other at the next meetin'."

"Of course."

He did not want anything more than that. No personal connection. It had been just a rare kindness he offered her. "Well, thank ye. Thank ye so much."

He nodded. He was so big, his head brushed the low-hanging steam lamp when he went out.

Livie closed down relentlessly on the ache inside her, and went home.

Chapter Four

Benton did find Olivia Scrubwoman beautiful. He could not deny it, try though he might as he made his way to the start of his route. With her long, honey-colored hair—he remembered the taste of honey from long, long ago—her eyes that looked blue in one light and green in another, and her slim, strong body, she appealed to him in a way no woman had for time out of mind.

Even if he dismissed the pull her body exerted upon his, there was her face. Irregular in shape, roughly oval but with one brow higher than the other. A bold nose with a hook in it, and a crooked smile. Nothing there, if you took the features apart, to make him call her beautiful. But when he put it all together—

By God, he'd wanted to take her back to his room and make love to her till dawn. And as something inside him insisted, it would be *making love*, which was something else he'd never done before.

Oh, he'd been to the whores a few times, sure. A man had to, from time to time. But that was just a body function, wasn't it, like any other with no emotions involved. Besides, the women who had been condemned to the job of whore were such pitiful creatures, he could scarcely bear to add to their misery.

Men and women, in an ordinary way, did couple. Those in the movement for human rights encouraged it, for the human population needed to increase. To grow strong enough to one day—probably not in Benton's lifetime—rise up and overthrow their masters.

It was considered a duty to reproduce. He might tell himself that in order to excuse a pursuit of Olivia. He wasn't quite stupid enough to believe it.

He made his way to the start of his route, passing others bent upon the same business and giving them nods. It wasn't raining quite as hard tonight, just a gentle patter that fell onto his head and shoulders and made patterns in the mud that coated the stones underfoot.

League was an old town and constructed mostly of stone. Once it had possessed another name. Few Cities yet survived on the planet—there were said to be a scant number on the other side of the world, so isolated they, like League, each had their own ruler and system of government.

Travel, with the sea now so wild, was near impossible and communication difficult. Men had constructed boats and tried for escape, thinking life elsewhere had to be better and easier, though they'd been assured it rained everywhere, globe-wide.

To Benton's knowledge, every boat had been lost, torn apart on the heavy seas. If any had reached their destinations, they had not returned to tell of it. Captured by foreign governments? Impounded? Killed? The other Cities might be worse than League, though he found that hard to warrant.

For all the difficulty and hopelessness of his life, he loved this city. Loved the bones—or stones—of it deep beneath the mud. His family had lived here for generations, perhaps tens of generations.

He just wished, to the roots of his soul, men could

take it back.

He reached his first lamp post and shimmied up, hands inured to the feel of the cold metal. Nose to the smell of the coal vapors. He had acquired a method and had his flint clutched between his teeth when he climbed. His pack—soft cloth—on his back contained spare parts, wicks and metal screws, all he would need to perform simple repairs on the spot, along with the snuff.

He raised the little door in the side of the glass, turned the thumb screw, and struck the flint. Light flared with a wisp of steam. He adjusted the height of the flame, closed the hatch, and backed down.

Suddenly Olivia was there in his head again. It seemed she meant to walk the stones with him tonight.

When had he first noticed her? Right away when she'd joined the meetings, if he was honest. A man could not help but notice. She'd come sporadically at first and sat in the corner, saying little. Listening. After a while, her impatience had begun to show. She'd hoped for more. Hoped for a miracle.

They always did.

He'd kept his eyes mostly away from her, because he didn't like to overstep himself. At least that was the excuse he used. Maybe because he was afraid—

Of what? Speaking to a woman? No, not that. Something else. Feeling a connection. Because connections could hurt.

But when he'd followed her and that ass Danny from the last meeting, seen Danny hitting on her, for there could be no question it was what he'd been doing, his emotions had taken over.

Damn his emotions.

He saw again the way she had looked at him there

in the noisy tavern. Those big, troubled eyes hiding her pain. She sought to disguise it just the way he did. He could feel that right through the skin of her poor, abraded hands.

*Can I see ye again?*

He heard her voice clear as a bell in his ear as he climbed his second light pole. One hundred-odd more of them on his route and—

His fingers slipped and, all the way up under the glass globe, he nearly fell. By God, he had to pay attention and couldn't be thinking of—

Olivia.

Footsteps sounded on the street below him as a pair of Police Dogs passed. Beagles they were, a matched pair, and they stepped in time, their boots squelching in the mud. Both wore the blue uniform, well-buttoned up, and the domed helmet. One had a cluster of mechanical parts visible at the back of his neck, peeking out beneath the headgear. The other lacked an ear.

They glanced up at Benton, clinging so perilously to his pole, as they passed by. They made up part of the ordinary force but would not hesitate to report any misdoings to the Grey Guard.

Watch dogs, Benton thought, but the slur did not quite allay his uneasiness.

Eyes were everywhere.

*Can I see ye again?*

The appeal in her gaze. The need that had flowed to him through her hands.

What had she meant by that?

Like a fool, he had answered that of course they would see one another at future meetings.

That was not what she'd meant.

Why had he failed to respond to her overture? For that surely it had been. Well, he had responded, if only inwardly.

That was what frightened him. Instinct told him that if he saw Olivia again, he might form a connection with her, one so deep that, were it broken, it could well destroy him.

And, he asked himself as he walked to his next post and shimmied up it, was he such a coward? Humans took that chance every day. By God, they even had children with their mates.

And he had seen what happened to them when they lost those mates.

He had to stop thinking about her. He should cease attending the meetings, if it meant seeing her there. The meetings weren't earning him anything anyway, save frustration. Only, attending them made it seem like he was making an effort at resistance, however futile.

His route turned a corner into a more prosperous street. Here were a number of gentlemen's clubs and gaming dens, and groups of animals walked the cobbles. They would be far more numerous later when he snuffed the lights out again.

A group of well-dressed Foxes passed him by, talking together in their high, yippy voices. The elegance of their attire, satin and brocade in a rainbow of colors, matched that of their glorious fur and cast Benton into muddy obscurity. Unlike the Beagles, they did not glance at him. He did not exist for them beyond being a duty-bound fixture that enabled the other fixtures in their world to operate.

Ironic, for they were the fixtures, mechanicals. Things. But the world had been inverted to place them at the top.

By one man's hand.

*What would happen if the Lord High died?*

Yes, what would happen?

There were assassins in their world. Highly-trained Tigers and Panthers. But if any man went to them with such a request, he would find himself in a dungeon and lying beneath heated irons before he could draw breath.

Benton had once seen an assassin. A Panther he had been, clad all in black to match his fur, only his eyes glowing amber. He'd carried a number of weapons, though it was whispered the assassins' preferred method of killing was the claw. The mechanical in question had been death itself, moving like a shadow.

Benton had to stop thinking of such things, had to stop thinking at all, and attend to his work. In all else lay disaster.

\*\*\*\*

The next meeting, according to word passed on the street with great discretion and caution, was to take place in the back room of the laundry on Kettle Street. Livie looked forward to it more than she should, and not because she felt eager for sedition.

It was Saturday, and she'd not seen Benton since the tavern.

Not that she expected much to come from any encounter with him. He'd made himself clear. Only, she found she wanted the pleasure of seeing him, though why she should count that such a pleasure, she could not say.

Big and hulking, with those broad bones and mud-brown eyes, he was no girl's dream. If girls still dreamed, which Livie very much doubted.

The back room of the laundry, where they were

allowed to gather, smelled of carbolic soap and damp, with an underlying reek of coal smoke. If Livie could think of a job worse than her own, it would be an assignment to such a place. Back-breaking labor and no escape from being wet. At least, not unless one counted the drying room where enormous fires were set.

Nothing dried out in the rain.

Livie did her own laundry but rarely in the small sink at home, washing the things out and hanging them to dry while she slept. She didn't possess many garments. What she had were faded, stained from the mud, and torn from scrubbing on all fours. She, too, used carbolic soap to battle the lice.

Members flitted in to the meeting, slipping through the back door in ones or twos, but Benton did not arrive. Livie tried to harness her disappointment. Had he decided to avoid her after what had taken place between them at the tavern? But, what had taken place?

He'd held her hands, only. Lent her a little comfort.

No, it had been more than that.

Her heart leaped every time someone else came in, only to fall again. Billy Spade began the meeting, and Livie did her best to pay attention.

There were rumors that rents were going to rise. So far it was only a rumor, but in the past such rumblings had been known to prove true, so they must attempt to prepare accordingly.

Prepare how? Asked Margie Cookwoman, desperation clear in her voice. She was already so far behind on her rent she had no hope of ever catching up. She could not afford an increase.

None of them could. Not unless their pay was also set to go up, which it wasn't.

And where would the increased revenue go, asked Pauly. To the Lord High, that was where. And he would distribute it to his Leagues, where it would serve to increase the wealth of those who already lived in luxury. So they could buy more finery, new carriages, and clocks, feathers for their hats and shiny boots and—

The door of the room snicked open. Benton sidled in.

He moved quietly for so large a man. He paused just inside the door to look around, and Livie willed him to take the empty space on the bench beside her.

He didn't, but sat in the corner.

The meeting droned on, members reciting their grievances. Livie failed to listen.

He had come. It seemed all out of proportion significant.

Someone had brought crackers and cold herb water to the meeting, situating them at the back of the room. Under cover of helping herself to a share, Livie rose and, pretending at being casual, took the seat next to Benton.

He did not react, just continued to sit with his big hands clasped between his knees. She wished he would touch her hands again, but he made no such move. She nibbled her cracker—stale—and pretended to listen to the discussion.

The things she might say to Benton ran through her head. All manner of things. She should make it casual, offhand. Ask him how he was doing. Keep it impersonal.

Instead, when the meeting paused to allow everyone a chance for refreshments, she turned to him and said, "I didn't think ye would come."

Emotions moved through his mud-colored eyes, but he did not evade her glance.

"I almost didn't. Olivia—we need to talk."

"Yes." Yes, she wanted to talk with him. Be with him. "The tavern, after?"

"Too noisy there. Do ye work tomorrow?"

Sunday. "No. Do ye?"

"No. they put the trainees on, for Sundays. It's called the day of death."

"Oh, goodness, why?"

"Many of them slip and fall."

"And ye never have?"

"I've fallen a few times. I'm pretty big and can absorb the impact. The first time it happened I was still a trainee and I thought I was dead."

He was talking to her, actually talking.

"Oh?"

"I hit my head on the cobbles, see? And I lay there in the mud thinkin'—*damn, I hoped the afterlife would be better, but it smells just the same as regular life.*"

Livie found herself smiling, leaning in to his company. "Is it easy to fall?"

"Very easy. Everythin's wet—the metal poles, the fixture, your hands. But knowin' death awaits has a way of heightenin' a man's reactions."

"Ye must be careful." Livie laid her hand on his arm. Only the tattered fabric of his coat sleeve, true, and not his skin, which she recalled had been warm, and felt good.

He stared at her hand lying there. It looked almost obscene, so red and chafed. But he did not pull away.

"Want to meet tomorrow?" he asked almost diffidently. "At the heroes' statue, the one by the river. What time is too early?"

No time was too early. "I'm used to risin' before

50

dawn."

"Ye should sleep in tomorrow, then. Say ten o'clock?"

"If that's good for ye. Or nine."

"Nine, then. I'll bring a breakfast. It won't be much."

She didn't care. She would be seeing him. Tomorrow.

Her whole world had changed. He wanted to talk with her. It did not occur to her to wonder what he wanted to discuss.

When the meeting resumed, she stayed beside him, though she removed her hand from his sleeve, folded it away with its mate as if it disgraced her. She could smell him—the scent of coal smoke, strong, coming off his coat. A tinge of damp. Another scent uniquely his. It seemed such an intimate thing, to smell another human.

They were basic creatures when it came down to it, weren't they? Was that not what the Lord High tried to emphasize by placing all the mechanicals above them? They ate and breathed and shat and worked and made love, all wallowing in the mud of their world, without airs or graces. Organic to the core.

Was it the organic part of her that was so attracted to this man? An impulse even the Lord High could not conquer?

After the meeting, he walked her to her house, an act that thrilled her so deeply she lacked words for it. As she'd failed to do to Danny Barman, she invited, "Would ye like to come up?"

What would happen if he did? They would talk and talk. Would he touch her? Would she touch him? Would he spend the night?

*Please come up*, she willed.

But he shook his head. "Best not. See ye tomorrow."

She watched him walk away, a hulking figure, a moving mountain. He had his barriers up.

At that moment in time, Livie felt utterly incapable of scaling them.

Chapter Five

The heroes' statue, a monument raised to honor the architects of a minor human uprising back after the Great Killing, had been broken so severely it no longer resembled people, just blobs of stone. Groups of Foxes and Ferrets out on the prowl and even some Police Dogs, so it was rumored, threw stones at it on a regular basis, spat on it, and sometimes used it for purposes of tamping out their coal dust.

But everyone in the human population remembered what it was and used it as a kind of touchstone.

All the participants of that uprising, if Benton recalled correctly, had been killed, tortured to death, and their bodies hung from government buildings, after, so humans could see the extent of their wounds.

Martyrs, they had become.

There was another heroes' statue on the heights of the town, set out to honor another group of dissenters, equally mutilated.

But here beside the river there was still some struggling greenery amid the mud, and Benton liked to walk here when it didn't rain too hard.

This day seemed blessed. The rain had abated to little more than a mist and he thought he could begin to glimpse a haze of sun behind it.

He reached the statue ahead of Olivia and stood, almost hoping she would not come. Better that way, perhaps. Cut off cold whatever threatened to exist between them.

Failing that, he needed to talk to her. Set things straight between them. For there were feelings, at least on his part. And he must convince her—himself—they should not explore any feelings, for in that direction lay only hurt.

He saw her coming with her long, tall strides up along the river walk, the weak light igniting her hair. Lovely hair. She wore her old gray coat with the mud stains around the hem, and the spattered shoes. But her gaze located and clung to him.

His heart rose.

See, this was why they should not associate with one another. He had to make it clear—

She reached him and smiled, that crooked smile that lit her eyes. Some of his good intentions died a swift death.

"Good mornin', Benton."

"Good mornin', Olivia."

"Do ye want to walk?"

"Yes, since it's not rainin' too hard."

"It's barely rainin' at all." He could tell by the lilt of gladness in her voice how her heart rose. As did his own.

"Which way?" he asked.

"Doesn't matter."

They walked. After ten paces she looped her arm through his, and he did not pull away. Another shred of resistance died.

Other couples were out walking, it being a cost-free entertainment. Mechanicals were also in evidence, the river front being one of those areas considered open to all. The mechanicals crept along in carriages exchanging greetings, or strolled in groups according to their League—a cluster of elegant Cats nodding at other Cats. Foxes who, by the look of them, hadn't been home all night.

"Did ye get any sleep?" Olivia asked. "Ye worked last night, yes?"

"I closed my eyes for a few minutes. I'm all right. Not too tired." He didn't feel tired at all in her company. Energized.

"It always feels so good havin' a whole day off. Though it tends to go by quickly."

"Yes." He folded his hand over hers where it curled around his arm. Protection, he told himself, rather than possession.

She was not his. By God, *he* was barely his. That was one of the problems in forming attachments. How did people find the courage for anything so perilous?

The rain, rather than falling, gathered on their skin, heavy with the scent of coal smoke. The City and the majority of its inhabitants ran on steam, which in turn ran on coal. Still, it was a gift of a day, and the number of individuals out and about proved as many as possible meant to take advantage.

"Do ye ever try to imagine," Olivia asked all at once, "what it was like—before?"

"Before the Killing, d'ye mean?" Benton drew a breath. He did, though that, just like finding a companion for his life, seemed an exercise in futility. "Sometimes."

"It must have been a little like this, only more so, if that makes sense." She wrapped her arm more tightly around his. "With more sunshine."

"And fewer animals." To Benton's own surprise, he gave a soft laugh. "And those there were would, by and large, be smaller and runnin' about on all fours."

"Have ye ever seen sunshine?" She gazed up at him, her eyes wide. "I mean, full on."

"No. Have ye?"

"No. But—it's strange—I can imagine it. Sometimes it's sunny in my dreams."

And there was a sad statement. If they could only have sunlight in their dreams—

"I seem to remember it," he admitted, "from when I was a small boy, though I know that can't be true. Perhaps it is but imagination."

"Atavistic memory."

"Eh?"

"Passed down from our ancestors. Imagine—they knew sunlight. A world that wasn't all mud and damp. All debt and sorrow."

He did not know what to say to that. Through the connection of their arms, wound together, he seemed able to feel her emotions, and he very much wanted to keep them elevated.

"People would walk around all the time like this," she chattered on, "in sunlight. Takin' it for granted. They must have been so happy."

"Ah, maybe. People bein' people, rarely seem to realize when they're happy."

She slanted another of those looks at him. Swift, confiding. "What's the happiest ye've ever been?"

*Right now.* But he couldn't tell her that, could he? Even if it were true. He shook his head helplessly.

She stopped walking and turned to face him. They were as near alone as might be, the river flowing beside them in its muddy bed, gurgling as it went. A few trees still stood here, their leaves dripping with wet.

She clutched both his hands, much the way he had hers back in the tavern, and she looked—well, more than beautiful with the rain beaded on her hair and her eyes gazing into him.

His whole body tensed. Something was coming, though he did not know what.

"Kiss me, Benton."

"Eh?"

"I want to know how it feels. I want to know how it might have been for our ancestors who took life for granted. Will ye please kiss me, and make this day perfect?"

Had she never been kissed? Or was it that she'd never been kissed out under what passed for a balmy sky?

He should not. A boundary, that was, and one he had determined not to cross. Wasn't that why he'd called her here today, to make it clear they could not be?

As he hesitated, her eyes grew larger. She leaned into him, pressing their joined hands against his chest. She was tall, but he was taller, and she had to reach up to press her mouth to his.

By heaven. By heaven!

His mind stuttered just like a steam lamp before it meant to blow. Sparks of light everywhere and a feeling of danger. Soft, her lips were, so soft and damp with the rain. They clung to his and she tasted him. Tasted him just as he tasted her.

Sweetness.

The force of it very nearly took him to his knees. A great wave of sensation unfurled and rushed through him from their joined lips, unstoppable.

See, this was why he knew he should not kiss her.

Why he should not see her.

But that was his brain talking, the sensible part of him. Now his body came to the fore, insistent on having its say.

He groaned and freed his hands from hers, but only so he could wrap them around her shoulders and draw her closer. Close into him.

The kiss did not cease but changed from something tentative that asked a question to something more. A demand which Olivia answered, parting her lips to him. Letting him in.

Oh, God, such bliss. He'd been right, back in the tavern. He needed to take her home and make love to her.

Would she let him?

"Olivia." Somehow he found the strength to end the kiss and look into her eyes. Impossibly wide they were, and filled with the same emotions he felt.

Dangerous ground, and his world seemed to rock beneath him.

"Come home with me," she whispered, and he closed his eyes, seeking for strength.

\*\*\*\*

Olivia leaned into the man who had his arms wrapped around her and gazed into his face. He had his eyes closed like someone fighting an inner battle, and nothing prevented her looking her fill. That broad, un-handsome face that appealed to her so strongly, mist gathered on his skin, on the hair that grew along his jaw, and beaded on the long, dark eyelashes. His lips that she'd just kissed. Looking at them made her want to taste them again. Who would imagine he might taste so good?

He could not say he didn't want her. With her body pressed to his and her arms stretched around his neck, she could feel that he did.

He fit with her, and that was good. He would fit her even better up in her room.

The battle fought, he opened his eyes. Out here in the light, his eyes weren't just the color of mud. They were light brown with other colors in them. Green and gold like hidden sunlight.

"Olivia. Honey." His broad-palmed hands caressed her back, moving up and down. "We shouldn't. It's what I meant to tell ye, today. A relationship—well, it can only end in hurt, can't it?"

"Can it?"

"Yes. Openin' oneself up to another person—"

"But there might be a great deal of pleasure first, right? I've had so little pleasure." Starved for it she was. And she had him, here.

"The thing is, if we open ourselves up to it, will the hurt outweigh the pleasure?"

"I don't know. I think I want to find out." She'd never before done anything like this, invited a male in. Opened her doors to him. She didn't know why it should be him, except—

"I trust ye," she told him. "Not to hurt me."

"Olivia, honey, there's always hurt."

Yes, it was a rule—no, a component of their lives.

"I don't care."

"Ye might, later."

For answer, she kissed him again. Sucked on one of his lips and then the other. Coaxed his tongue into her mouth.

Time went away. Even in a city full of clocks, it did. The carriages continued to trundle past on the roadway. Voices sounded close by. Olivia knew none of it save the warmth of him that spread to her.

She breathed into him, "Please."

"Which way?"

They went hand in hand, turning back the way they had come against the tide of traffic. Olivia had never before felt anything like this, as if she could no longer sense the familiar cobbles beneath her feet, as if her heart had expanded within her and somehow carried her above the surface of the earth.

A superlative kind of feeling, she decided.

They did not speak. When they entered her neighborhood and paused at her house, he pulled back.

"Olivia. Olivia, I wanted to tell ye—"

"Come inside and tell me, then. Ye can tell me anythin'."

"There are lines we should not cross in life because it is not wise. This is one of them."

"Ye're right. But like I said, I don't care."

She opened the door and waited. If he followed her over the threshold into the cold and muddy hallway, she would know joy. If not, despair.

Despair that might last her a lifetime.

He stepped in behind her, quietly for such a big man. She kept moving, afraid if she did not he would balk. Up the narrow stairs that clattered beneath their feet. To her door.

Swiftly, swiftly she unlocked it and towed him in. The place was dim, with no window. Stuffy, yet cold.

"It smells of ye," he said.

"Is that good?"

"Yes. Oh, yes."

Yet he stood where he was just inside the door. More by feel than anything else, she began unfastening his buttons. "Give me your coat. I'll hang it up."

He shrugged out of the garment. She shed her own coat also. There was nowhere to sit except the bed. She towed him there and they perched side by side on the edge of the mattress.

He took her hands the way he had in the tavern, caressing. Olivia's whole body responded.

"I want to have my say, Olivia."

"All right."

"This—a relationship between us—is not a good idea."

"So ye said. But why?"

"Ye must know why. Givin' oneself to another person, openin' up that way—well, it means more struggle, doesn't it? It ends in hurt."

He seemed very certain of that. "Does it have to?"

"From what I've seen. Maybe I'm not brave enough to take the chance."

Olivia said nothing. Desperation washed over her in a staggering wave.

For several moments they sat in silence, only their hands touching. Then she said, "We are offered so little in this life. Why refuse what is offered?"

"Because it's wise."

"Or very, very foolish."

Slowly she freed her work-worn hands from his grasp. Raised them to the front of his shirt and began to unbutton it. Beneath, his skin felt warm.

*Warm.*

"Olivia, if ye do that, I can't say what will happen."

"That's all right."

She could.

Chapter Six

If madness was the taste of Benton upon Olivia's tongue, the feel of him when she got him out of his clothing, then she craved madness. In fact, it seemed she'd been awaiting just such a madness all her life.

She could not see him well, even after her eyes adjusted to the gloom. But, oh, she could feel him. The heat of him, and the breath issuing from his chest which was covered in damp hair. The strength of him. His body so different from hers.

Perhaps the Cats were right about humans. They were crass, organic beings after all. Driven by their base impulses. She did feel driven.

At least Benton stopped protesting after she pushed him down onto the bed. Stopped protesting and began participating enthusiastically. He seemed to enjoy touching her as much as she liked touching him, once their clothing came away. Those broad, strong hands of his were everywhere. At her waist, encircling her back. Up and down her legs. At her breasts.

It felt so good, she had no words for it.

She stretched her body atop his and kissed him, alive to every sensation. If the kisses out on the street had been good, these were better. Deeper. Accompanied by wordless sounds.

He buried his fingers in her hair and she could tell how he reveled in it.

*He likes my hair.*

He lifted her easily and moved his mouth from her lips to her breast, the motion of his lips questing, stoking her madness.

*He likes my breasts.*

Very, very gently he flipped her onto the narrow mattress and rose up over her, seeming to gaze at her a moment, though she could not guess what he saw, before he kissed his way from her breasts downward.

Up and down her legs where his hands had already been. Hovering between them so she felt his breath at her most private place. Warm.

"May I, Olivia?" His voice came in a harsh whisper and she could tell he felt what she did, this staggering arousal.

"Anythin'."

He urged her thighs apart. Lowered his mouth there. His lips and tongue, persuasive, coaxed her to surrender to him, to offer up the last bits of trust she had not already granted him. Her reward came in a rush that left her gasping and made her see stars.

Oh! Oh, was this what it meant to be alive?

When he made his way back up her body to kiss her, she wrapped her hands around him. Hard, he was, and apart from what he'd just given her, the best thing she'd ever felt.

She withdrew her mouth from his to say, "I want to taste ye, too."

His only reply came in a woodless groan, one she took for approval.

What followed would have shattered her world had it not already been shattered. Strong he was in her mouth, and responsive to her tongue's caress. He moved in and out of her, the movement so thrilling she felt that pleasurable tension grow inside her once again.

When he seized her head and said, "Honey, darlin', I'm goin' to—"

She made a wordless sound of assent. He flooded her mouth with liquid warmth, the taste so wild and primitive she nearly convulsed again.

A part of him. Now inside her. As it was meant to be.

"I'm sorry," he said once he'd drawn her up into his arms. "I'm sorry. I didn't mean to—"

"I liked it." Was that wrong of her to say? After what had just taken place, was there room for anything but truth between them?

He laughed unsteadily and she loved the way that sounded there in the semi-dark. No longer alone.

Oh, she'd been so alone. Not even knowing how alone.

"Hold me. Just hold me," she begged.

They clutched one another, arms wrapped tight. She could hear his heart beneath her ear, thudding before settling down to a peaceful rhythm. So strong, he was.

"Benton." She stretched up from her place on his chest, brushed her lips lightly across his. Once. Twice. "I like the way ye taste. Is that wrong?"

He huffed and answered, "Ye're askin' me what's right and wrong? Damned if I know. I like the way ye taste too, darlin'." He nuzzled her ear. "And though I didn't intend to release myself that way, it's probably better than inside ye."

"Ye were inside me."

"I mean—" Very gently his fingers brushed her between her legs. Lingered. "That's how ye get a babe."

"Yes."

"So, better—"

"Does it feel as good for ye as it does for me when ye kiss me there?" She felt so inadequate on the subject, she who usually considered herself streetwise.

"Yes. Oh, yes."

"Like nothin' else?"

"Like nothin' else."

"No wonder people do it."

"No wonder. Olivia, I want to tell ye—ye be beautiful."

She did not know how to respond to that. She said nothing.

"Ye have beautiful hair. Beautiful breasts. I like everythin' about ye."

"I like everythin' about ye, also."

"I'm nothin' but a big ox. There's nothin'—"

"Hush." She kissed him to silence him. "Ye be perfect. Understand?"

*Perfect for me.*

They dozed and woke to pleasure one another again. This time she made her way down his body and coaxed him inside her mouth to a repeat of what he'd given her before. So close was she to shattering then, only his fingers were inside her before she flew apart. This, she thought after, this was belonging. This, how it was meant to be.

"Olivia," he said after a time, "I should—"

"Don't go. Please." She tightened her hold on him. "Stay."

He drew breath to speak. She didn't give him the chance. "I've never felt like this. So—so human. I mean, I've felt human in the way the Cats make us feel, lowly and worthless. Beneath them. But this, this is a powerful feelin'."

"It is."

"Ye don't have to work tonight, do ye? So stay with me."

\*\*\*\*

Benton doubted very much he had the strength required to rise out of that bed. His mind kept telling him he should leave, but that was mere lip service. His body told him other things.

Never had it spoken so loudly.

Yes, his body served him well when he was out on the streets braving the wet and cold, pushed almost beyond endurance in the course of his work. It rarely complained.

Now it insisted that this, only this, was its reward and all it wanted.

Olivia. She represented warmth and pleasure and sanctuary. And danger. He could lose himself to this woman. Losing her, in turn, would destroy him.

This, he knew instinctively. He was strong, yes. Not strong enough to bond with her and then part with her.

But perhaps it was already too late. Maybe they'd already bonded. Him, inside her mouth. Her welcoming him.

She stirred in his arms and her fingers danced down his chest, down his stomach. Wrapped around him.

"Umm," he half groaned. "Do ye want me again?"

"Only let me show ye."

Later, much later, they rose from the bed and, both starving, raided her stock of food for a meal. There wasn't much, and he wished he could help her procure more. Provide for her. Another ancient instinct.

Should he not be able to provide for his woman? The Cats had stolen that ability from mankind, a means of keeping them down. In so much debt there was nothing to spare. Nothing to gift.

Was Olivia his woman?

"Why are ye lookin' at me that way, Benton?"

She lounged on the bed only half dressed, eating a cracker, with her hair in a glorious tangle and her long legs stretched out.

"How am I lookin' at ye?"

She tipped her head to one side. "I can't quite say. Either as if ye're worried, or ye want another round of lovin'."

*Loving.*

"I think three is my limit."

"I bet not."

He laughed, startled by her guileless honesty. She had a way of doing that, surprising him and making him laugh.

"I am worried. This is dangerous ground we walk."

"Why do ye say that? So long as ye don't release yourself up inside me, we should be all right, yes?"

It wasn't the physical aspects that concerned him, or not *just* the physical aspects. Sure, it was a wondrous release. But his heart—

"It's dangerous because so many things in our world can go wrong."

"Ye're right. So we'd better enjoy it while we can, eh?"

Should he tell her? Tell her he feared he was falling in love with her so fast he might already be past saving? That he might have begun falling in love with her back during those meetings, just watching her, seeing the way she was, even before he'd touched her?

He never should have touched her.

She leaned forward, put her hand on his bare leg. Slid it upward. "Stay. The rest of the night till morning. Ye don't have to work. I do, but ye can leave when I go to the job. Let's make the most of it."

Already she did not want to let go of him. As he did not want to let go of her. That terrified him.

"I think I should go." Somehow, he forced the words past his lips.

She slid her hand still higher. A wicked light appeared in her eyes. "I think ye should come."

Instinct was a marvelous thing, as Olivia whispered sometime later. It must have been halfway through the night. She lay in his arms with her mouth at his ear.

"A while ago, I never knew what it meant to be with a man. Oh, I understood the ins and outs of it, if ye'll excuse the pun. But I didn't understand how knowin' could just come to a woman."

"Ye're wondrously good at it." He captured her chin gently—he always touched her gently—and turned her mouth so he could kiss her. "For a newbie."

"That's instinct for ye. It. just. Comes. Reachin'."

She punctuated each word with a little kiss on his lips and he was lost. Perhaps more precisely, he admitted he was lost.

"I'll admit," she went on artlessly, "I'd like to feel ye inside me. All of ye. But I suppose we shouldn't risk makin' a child."

"We shouldn't."

"The great size of ye—d'ye think ye would fit?"

"Yes." She was tight. His fingers told him that. But by God, he would fit.

See, though, this was where the danger lay. One intimacy led to another. Before you knew it—

"Never mind," she said comfortably. "Next time."

There should be no next time. To the root of his soul, he knew that. "Olivia—"

"Oh, I know it won't be easy findin' opportunities with your schedule and mine. But there's always Sundays. I don't see why we shouldn't spend every Sunday like this."

*Damn right*, his body screamed.

*Therein lies eventual ruination*, insisted his brain.

She granted him another of those light kisses. "It will give me a reason to live till Sunday."

Him too, God help him.

****

It rained hard when he reported for work Monday night, cold drops pelting down like nails. Some god's vengeance, he thought as he reached the start of his route, isolated amid the noise of the onslaught.

When it rained this hard, sometimes the lamps did not want to light. They sputtered after he turned the screw, and if enough of the coal-produced gas built up, that was when you could have an explosion. He'd seen men killed.

As he approached his first target, he told himself to be careful. Not easy, when all he could think of was—

*Olivia.*

It had been how many hours since he'd parted from her? And he could still feel her hands on him. Feel her lips on him. He ached for her.

She had gone to work today, parting from him with still more kisses. He worked tonight. No meeting of the Freedom Seekers scheduled, so no hope of laying eyes on her.

He shouldn't mind. He should be glad of a breather and a chance for sanity to set in, because what had happened between them yesterday—

Well, it had been madness.

He shimmied up the first pole, his knees slipping on the wet metal, the flint clutched between his teeth.

If that had been madness, the insanity had not ebbed. Because he could still feel the texture of her nipple against his tongue. He could still taste her.

He lit the lamp and clung to the pole as a group of fashionable Cats walked by. They wore long cloaks with hoods and had a number of human attendants following them to keep their hems out of the mud. Other humans stepped sideways, holding umbrellas over the Cats' heads.

All the humans were wet to the skin. Just like him, and he'd only just begun his rounds.

He knew there was a certain hard justice to it. He knew that in the past men had often treated the animals in their charge with casual cruelty. Tossed cats out to fend for themselves. Tied dogs to a tree or a poor excuse for a shelter in all weathers. Confined dairy cows in their hundreds and worked horses to death.

What happened now might be considered payback.

In the past, mankind's only claim to superiority over his fellow creatures had been his intelligence. Now the Lord High had levelled that playing field. Those Cats down on the street were as intelligent as he was, even if it was artificial intelligence.

And they had metal claws.

Still, it rankled to watch his fellow humans scurrying along while the arrogant felines failed to so much as take notice of them or of the care they provided.

Something must be done about the Cats. What had Olivia said about curiosity?

Olivia, there she was in his head again.

Once the troop of Cats passed, he climbed down the pole and went on to his next. Made it up and down safely for the ensuing three or four before on the next he slipped, the wet fabric of his trousers losing their grip and letting him slither down. He managed to arrest the slide with the palms of his hands, but the rough metal of the corroded pole tore them.

He hung there, heart pounding, teeth gritted against the pain, telling himself how fortunate he was not to have fallen.

But was he fortunate? Here he clung—not worth so much as a glance from the passersby—with over a hundred more lamps to light, and shredded hands.

An awful state of being.

A new thought crept into his mind. *Maybe it would be better if I fell. Smashed on the ground. All this dread and struggle over.*

Another thought followed that one. *Then I'd never be able to touch Olivia again.*

Was she—the promise of her—worth living for? If so, he truly was in trouble because such powerful feelings put him in a perilous position. In debt to his own heart.

He went on, grimly now, intent upon finishing his rounds. And only the rain washed the blood from his hands.

Chapter Seven

"I'm sorry, Mistress Ferret. Truly I am."

Livie crouched on the floor of the tiled foyer, seeking to gather the pieces of the smashed bauble into her hands. She'd hoped the mistress of the house, Melia Ferret, would have failed to hear the commotion, but the thing had made an awful crash when Livie—scrubbing mud from the floor—had bumped a table upon which the bauble stood.

It had toppled in slow motion and though Livie stretched out a hand, she hadn't been able to catch it.

Mistress Melia drew herself up. Ferrets were a diminutive League. She was not much taller than a House Mouse, but she made up for it in indignation.

She wore a blood-red gown, gaudy but expensive enough that its price could have kept a human family for a year. It had lace at the neck and cuffs, and Mistress Melia wore a wig, one made of human hair, if Livie was not mistaken.

"Clumsy wretch!" she screamed at Livie. "Look what you've done."

"I didn't mean to. I bumped the table by accident."

"That was a gift. A gift from my mate!" When the Ferret raised her mechanical voice it took on a whine that hurt Livie's ears.

"Maybe it can be repaired." Livie stared at the pieces of porcelain in her hands. A round ball here, a curved stem there, all in a bilious shade of green. What had the thing been?

Most Ferrets, being of the thieving class, did not warrant human cleaners, but this pair must be important indeed, for their home was opulent and filled with fine furniture and trinkets. Ferrets, by and large, fenced what the Raccoons stole. Melia's mate, Master Pierre, likely directed a whole squad of them.

"And look," Melia screeched on, "you have not even got all the muddy prints up off the floor."

"Not yet, ma'am. I was workin' on that."

It was her fourth house of the day, and it was nearly six o'clock. She couldn't leave till she finished.

Master Pierre came out of the sitting room and into the foyer. Just Livie's luck that the hour was late enough for him to be at home.

"What is amiss?"

He had a sharp, overtly ferrety face with sleek tan fur and sharp dark eyes. Livie did not like him, had never liked him. Matching his mate, he stood upright, his sinuous body clad in a suit of puce-colored satin and knee britches.

"What has happened here?"

"Look what she did. Look what she did!"

He looked. His sharp face grew somehow sharper. "Did you break that, Scrubwoman?"

"Yes, sir. I did. I'm very sorry, but it was an accident."

Livie started to get up from her knees. Pierre Ferret struck out so swiftly she never saw the blow coming. His paw caught her on the cheek in a slap hard enough to knock her back down.

She landed with one cheek on the cold tiles, the

upper one stinging. "Oh!"

"I will report this. The value of the statue will come out of your wages."

Statue. Had it been a statue?

"Get up and get out of here."

"But, Pierre, the floor Is not clean."

"Finish, then, Scrubwoman, and go."

Livie dragged herself up, resisting the urge to put a hand to her stinging cheek. She finished scrubbing the floor, trying hard not to cry and only realized her cheek was bleeding where Pierre's claw had caught the skin when tiny red drops mixed with the mud.

Mistress Melia fled in the direction of the kitchen with the gathered pieces of the bauble. Master Pierre stood in the doorway of the parlor and watched Livie finish her work. Watched her don her coat, thin and inadequate against the wet. Watched her gather her bucket of scrubbing supplies and go.

Outside she stood on the street for a moment, stock still, trying to breathe. Rain poured down, falling so hard it bounced on the cobbles and threatened to slice through her clothing to the skin. She did not want to stand here and weep, but for the moment she didn't feel capable of anything else.

She hated her life.

That was a terrible thing to admit, because it was her life, damn it, and all she had, but despair gripped her so fiercely she wanted only to disappear from it, to cease pushing her way through these terrible days. To flee.

Nowhere to go. She had nowhere and almost nothing, no way to support herself if she broke free. There was a world beyond League City, but it was big and dark and wet and inhospitable. She did not know how she would survive out there.

Would Master Pierre report her as he'd threatened? That would mean being called up before a council of Cats to explain herself and perhaps accept punishment. The nature of that punishment was far-reaching. She might merely be required to pay for the bauble, which meant more debt, for she had no coin. It might mean imprisonment. Physical punishment. Torture.

Not for the sake of a bauble, surely?

She began walking slowly, directionless, through the rain. The punishment she received would depend on the whim of the council who heard Master Pierre's complaint. Cats could be capricious—they were so by nature. She could lose her position and then her room, which wasn't much, but still, her only haven. Survival balanced on so little—bumping into a table could destroy her life.

She hated that the mechanicals had such power and treated it so casually. With one wave of a mechanical paw, they could destroy her. And they wouldn't care.

The rain had washed away any tears she'd shed. She snuffled back the last of them and caught herself up.

Everything in her life wasn't bad. There had been Sunday. The almost-sunshine. The long conversation with Benton. What had come after.

But now, walking through the heavy gloom, Sunday seemed like a dream, hazy as if it had never happened.

It had.

All at once she longed for Benton so strongly, it shook her. Where was he now? Preparing to begin his rounds?

She ached to see him. More, she ached for the touch of his big hands, somehow so gentle. At her breast. At her thigh.

*Please*, she beseeched the very air around her. *Please tell me I'm not falling in love with Benton Lightman.*

She did not know that she believed in love. True, people did still form what they called marriages wherein they clung together, but it seemed to be an exercise in loyalty more than anything else.

She would not mind being loyal to Benton.

Couples did live together until one of them was imprisoned or perished. They brought children into the world, which only made things harder.

But it did raise the human population of the City, which so many protestors believed would eventually correct the imbalance.

It was so skewed now, it would take a long, long time to amend. Generations.

Was that what kept human couples together? The loyalty, the need to reproduce. There was also attraction. She had witnessed that in action often enough—in the taverns, especially. A quick, heedless, and somehow impulsively human thing.

By God, she'd now experienced it for herself. She and Benton—doing those things they had together, the intimacy of it without restraint or embarrassment. Was that intimacy what kept people bonded? It seemed closer to a truth.

But even that was not love.

She began to pass shops, most of them still open, and some clubs outside of which groups of Cats and Foxes gathered, all well-dressed and busy conversing. They did not so much as glance at her trudging along with her bucket and sopping clothing.

She reached the tavern on the corner where she needed to turn for her street, and hesitated. Light spilled out and voices. Music. Life. She wanted to go in.

She couldn't afford it, especially now. She must keep from going any deeper into debt in case she lost her job.

Yet a drink would steady her. And the alternative was worrying alone in her room.

She went in. The sound hit her first, a wall of it, and the scent of unwashed humanity liberally splashed with mud. The people crowding the tavern were all shabby, all poor. All alive.

She edged to the bar and set her bucket at her feet. "An ale, please."

The glass was put in front of her, the barman's gaze slipping over her face with what might be sympathy. When she scrabbled for coins, he shook his head. "On the house, love."

A simple act of kindness. Could it save her?

She turned and surveyed the room for a place to sit, nearly colliding with a large form behind her.

"Olivia?"

He backed off a step the better to eye her. Concern flooded his eyes, closely followed by consternation.

"What's happened to ye?" He raised a hand to her cheek. "Ye're bleedin'. And—have ye been cryin'?"

"Benton? What are ye doin' here?"

"I'm about to go to work. I have a few minutes. Come on."

He put an arm around her, and at that moment in time it was among the best things she'd ever felt. He scooped up her bucket in his other hand and led her to a corner. People parted for them to pass.

There were no empty tables but he leaned her against the wall and, still eyeing her with that concern, asked, "What's happened?"

She poured it all out to him, how she'd bumped the table and broken the bauble, the cruelty of her employers, and what would likely happen next.

"Ferrets?" he asked, frowning. "But they're all fencers. He likely stole that statue, or whatever it was."

"Doesn't matter. I'm responsible."

Very gently, Benton touched her face. "He's torn your cheek."

"I think his claw caught me when he knocked me down."

Anger stirred in Benton's eyes. "It's ugly. Ye'll likely have a scar. Can ye see an herbalist?"

"I don't have the coin."

He began to dig in his pocket.

"No, Benton—it will be all right. Only," she caught her breath, "if it does scar, will ye think less of me?"

"Why would I?"

She stared into his eyes. "Ye called me beautiful before, when we—"

"So ye are." The hard anger in his voice softened. "So ye'll always be."

He leaned forward and very gently dropped a kiss on her cheek. Her whole battered soul rose and strained toward him.

"Oh, God, Benton. I—" She caught a glimpse of his palm as he reached to cup her chin. "What's happened to your hand? Your palm is torn. Oh, goodness!"

He made a rueful face and showed her both his palms. Deeply abraded and raw, the scrapes had been cleaned but looked painful. "It happened last night. I lost my grip and slid down a pole."

"Ye need those bandaged. How can ye climb up dozens of poles with them like that?"

"Can't spare the time or—" She knew why he broke off. *Or the coin.* Yet he was willing to give her what he could not spare.

Was that love?

A smile tugged one corner of his generous mouth. "I decided a fortifyin' drink would do more good."

"Let me wrap them. We can use my underdress." She could not bear the thought of him using those torn hands to climb all night.

But he shook his head. "The poles are rough. The bandages would be in shreds before I complete half my rounds."

She caught his wrist, pressed her lips against one palm. Desire arose.

She wanted him again. Wanted all of him. But that was not love.

"I want to see ye, Benton. Be with ye. Do we have to wait till Sunday?"

"I can't see any other way."

"If I get called up before the Cat Council, if they imprison me—"

"That won't happen."

"It might. It does. Then I won't be able to see ye."

"Ye're worth more to them out workin' than in a cell."

"Ye can never tell what a Cat will do. I hate them, Benton. I hate them all."

For answer, he drew her into his arms. Held her there tight, the only comfort he had to give. They stood that way for several moments, the confusion of the tavern somehow separate from them, before he said regretfully, "I must get to work."

"Yes. No sense ye getting' in trouble." She drew back far enough to gaze into his face. "Ye will take care?"

"Yes."

She stretched up and kissed him, mouth pressed to mouth, and the desire simmering inside her flared.

*This man.* She did not know why him. The feeling simply was.

When the kiss ended, his eyes burned. "There's a meetin' Friday night. Will ye be there?"

"If I'm not in a cell."

"Ye won't be."

Olivia wished she believed it.

"Be careful out there. I—" She'd almost told him what she felt. What she thought she felt.

"I will be. See ye Friday then."

"And—Sunday?" She had to cling to that.

He nodded. "And Sunday."

He went out, leaving her thinking that maybe she could survive a while after all.

## Chapter Eight

A slow anger burned inside Benton as he began his route, enough to made him disregard the pain the rough poles inflicted on his raw hands as he climbed them. Olivia's pretty face, ripped. Torn by a Ferret's claw. And yes, she was pretty, her skin still smooth and soft.

And yes, there would be a scar.

The emotions that filled him as he set about his rounds included the anger—futile anger—and sorrow and helplessness. The desire to protect her. Did a man not have the right to protect his woman?

There were so many things wrong with that thought, he scarcely knew where to begin.

Was she his woman?

Just because they had pleasured each other for a day and a night—and sweet God how they had pleasured each other—did not mean he had any claim on her. He was her first experience with passion. That might well have gone to her head.

It didn't mean her eyes would not turn elsewhere. What was he, after all? Big, hulking, chained to his job which took place at an inconvenient time of day—otherwise ordinary.

She would find someone better, if she decided she wanted a man.

He could not even protect her from abuse by her employers or the dangers of the Council. To be fair, no man could. In the old days, before the Killing, it had been different. A man might take a woman for his wife and thereafter have the right to defend her.

To be sure, people still married, if not legally. And if not legally, it meant nothing save to those involved.

She was right, if she were hauled up before the Cat Council, anything could happen to her. And for all his tumultuous feelings, he could not prevent it.

It felt like the Cats stripped his very masculinity from him.

By the end of the night, his hands were once more torn and bleeding. He met Andy on a street corner, when he headed home. Since the incident with the Grey Guard, they had stopped meeting part way through their shift, but Andy halted him now.

"Benny, did ye hear?"

"Hear what?" His heart leaped. Had Olivia already been arrested? But Andy would have no way of knowing that.

"Georgie. He's been up before the Cat Council."

"Oh." Benton's heart sank. "Sentenced?"

"Aye."

"To prison?"

"Worse." Andy's brow wrinkled. "They're sendin' him to the mines."

Benton puffed out a breath. "No."

Since their world ran on steam and burned coal, it was a commodity in constant demand. The mines in the west, far from League, operated around the clock, were run by Donkeys, with little respite and no mercy. Conditions were brutal and men assigned there were worked to death.

No one ever returned.

He said to Andy, "That seems harsh."

Andy shrugged. "They need men. All the time."

"Yes." Benton thought about it, and shivered. "What about Petie?"

"Haven't heard. Maybe he hasn't been up before the Council yet. I don't doubt he'll get the same."

Suddenly Benton's stinging palms didn't hurt so badly.

There were worse things. At least he could look forward to Sunday. If Olivia did not get arrested.

At least they did not send women to the mines.

Mankind had to do something to defend their world, wrest control of it back into their own hands. If only he knew how.

****

The hammer did not fall the next day, Wednesday, even though Livie dreaded it would. She went through her day as usual, cleaned her four houses, went home at the end of it.

Not till the next morning did she receive the demand, brought by a Squirrel messenger who stood at her door.

"Livie Scrubwoman? You are required to report to the Grand Council at eleven a. m. this morning. Your assignments will be taken by the Sunday cleaner."

Olivia's heart fell so drastically, her stomach turned.

The Grand Council Chamber was adjacent to the palace where lived the Lord High. It would take her a good while to walk there.

She might never return.

Once the Squirrel left, she glanced around her little room, wondering what would happen to her things if she did not return. She certainly did not have much. Perhaps they would fall to whoever inherited her quarters if she went to prison, just as her job would likely go permanently to her Sunday relief cleaner.

Suddenly the tiny, grim room seemed unbearably precious to her. Home. Everything, it seemed, was relative, and the life she'd lately lamented seemed dear. She knew it. She understood it.

Could she get word to Benton that she'd been summoned? Would he care?

Yes, he would care. She'd seen the concern in his eyes when they met at the tavern. Glimpsed his fear for her.

He'd tried to reassure her, but he'd feared this.

She wasn't used to having time on her hands and didn't know what to do with it. She dressed in her cleanest clothes, pinned up her hair, and then started walking.

It rained lightly but steadily, and she wished she could afford a cab—just so she wouldn't arrive dripping wet. Somehow she felt it important to make a good impression at the Chamber.

It—and the palace—lay at the center of town, up on a hill. Built on an open square, the building was a square itself, made of old stone, and housed not only the Cat Council but the entire government. To one side, so it was rumored, stood the jail, with the dungeons and torture chambers beneath.

Would she end up there? A shiver traced its way down Livie's back like a cold raindrop. Fear near paralyzed her.

A clock set upon a tower at one corner of the complex said it was ten-thirty. She had time to locate the Council Chamber and present herself on time.

The area was busy, swarming with mechanicals of every description. They hurried around, some leaving the buildings and some hurrying in. The majority were Cats—sleek Cats, luxuriously furred Cats, some dressed in the latest fashion and some in long, gray robes. All shared an air of self-importance as if they conducted official business of great significance. They bore their various mechanical alternations and augmentations with what looked like pride.

A haze of coal smoke mixed with rain and steam tainted the air hanging like a cloud, and it had stained the stone of the buildings. It tasted like foreboding on Livie's tongue.

She did not want to enter that building. She wanted to run. If she did, officers would be sent out to locate and capture her. Possibly the Grey Guard.

She could see a group of them now, standing at the top of the stairs in their magnificent gray cloaks, speaking together. They wore weapons—great, shining swords. But their true weapons were their metal teeth and claws.

If a Ferret's claws had done enough damage to tear her face and leave a scar, what might a Wolf's do?

She climbed the stairs, counting them as she did so. Ten, twenty. Forty. Fifty-five. A pair of watch Dogs stood at the top, flanking the great doors. They were Dobermans, a matched set.

"Name?" growled the one on the left as the other put out a mechanical arm to bar Livie's way.

"Livie Scrubwoman."

The Doberman consulted some list secured in his artificial intelligence. "Report to the main Council Chamber. Straight ahead."

"Thank ye."

His companion lowered his arm. Livie went in.

Slightly more order reigned inside than out. More Dogs stood around directing people, but most of those here were Cats. A few Squirrels, hurrying about, a Fox lounging in the corner.

Livie could not see Mistress Melia or Master Pierre anywhere. She wondered if they'd turn up.

All this for a broken bauble, one quite likely stolen.

She passed into the inner chamber, feeling quite small and very much alone. Up to now, she'd lived a careful life, keeping herself out of trouble. The boldest thing she'd ever done was join the meetings that preached sedition.

That and giving herself to Benton.

Oh, how she wished he were here now. But she wouldn't want to share her danger with him. She cared about him, didn't she?

Oh, yes.

Benches filled the rear of the chamber, many already crowded with animals of every description. The humans, very much a minority, ranged to one side, and that was where Livie headed.

A Squirrel scribe stood there, backed by what must be the bailiff, an enormous brown Bear with mechanical eyes. Livie wondered who would dare to defy him.

"Name?" the Squirrel squeaked at her, and she gave it. "Sit."

The others seated on the benches did not look at her when she joined them. One sweeping glance told her they all appeared the way she felt. Fearful. Isolated.

Three Cats entered the chamber from a side door and took their places behind an elevated table at the head of the room. All wore gray robes. They looked superior and very elegant.

Two females and a single Tom. Livie had heard that Toms were more merciful than their counterparts—if only because they remained more indifferent—but she did not know if she believed it.

If she could separate her fear from her discernment, she would have to admit that all three of these Cats were beautiful. The female on the left was mostly white, long-haired with a few streaks of gray. Her one visible eye, the other being concealed behind a mechanical eyepiece, was blue.

The Tom, in contrast, was black and looked like a smaller version of a panther. His whiskers were long and luxurious, one of his arms partly mechanical. His eyes were golden.

The other female, a short-hair, had fur of dove gray that from a distance looked like velvet. Both her ears and part of the top of her head had been replaced by mechanical apparatus.

These three held Livie's fate in their paws.

As soon as they assumed their places, the Bear lumbered forward to take a stance beside them.

Most Bears worked as guards at the smoking clubs and gaming hells—what would, in the old days, have been called bouncers for some unknown reason—or so it was rumored out in the wilderness beyond the walls of the City. There had been a few instances in recent years when irate humans had tried to set fire to such places, and it had been decided something more than guard Dogs were required.

Livie wondered how this Bear had achieved such an elevated position. He looked almost bored, as if he had seen and heard it all. She imagined he had.

The white Cat called the chamber to order, not bothering to introduce herself or her colleagues, and procedures began. Several humans were ahead of Livie. They were required to step forward. Their cases were heard with disturbing briefness and sentences pronounced.

Such sentences! One woman, accused of insulting her employer, who was a member of the Grey Guard, was sentenced to three days in jail. She cried, "But what of my children? They will be alone!"

With a wave of the Tom Cat's paw, she was ushered aside.

Two other women, consistently late for their jobs, were dismissed with severe warnings. Livie began to hope. But then came the woman accused of stealing from a shop. The shop owner—a Chipmunk—was there to testify.

The Cats listened briefly to the shopkeeper and not at all to the accused woman before her sentence was pronounced.

"To the dungeons," The Tom said carelessly.

"No!" The woman howled and every human in the room sat up straighter.

"You have used your hand to steal," the shorthaired Cat accused. "Now we shall see how much pain your hand can endure."

The shrieking woman was hauled off by two Alsatians under the watchful eye of the Bear.

"Livie Scrubwoman!"

Livie's knees trembled beneath her as she rose and stepped forward. She felt small and very shabby. Not one of the three Cats so much as glanced at her.

From nowhere, Pierre Ferret materialized. So crowded was the chamber, Livie hadn't realized he was there.

He stood serious and elegant in a mustard-colored satin coat and ivory knee britches. The white Cat addressed him. "Master Pierre, you accuse this woman, a scrubber at your home, of breaking a precious artifact?"

"I do, Madame Council Cat."

"How did this occur?"

"It was an accident," Livie said.

The white Cat's blue eye touched on her. "You will speak when given permission. Now, Master Pierre, how did this occur?"

"Carelessness."

The Tom Cat stirred impatiently, as if he tired of sitting there or protested having his time wasted. The shorthair did not react.

"I was cleanin'," Livie said, "and bumped the table where—"

The white Cat's gaze became a cold glare. "Are you incapable of being silent?"

Livie shook her head.

The shorthair asked Pierre, "What is the value of the broken item?"

"Invaluable, Mistress Council Cat. A treasured family heirloom."

The shorthair tutted, her mechanical voice box stuttering slightly. The white Cat looked at Livie. "You may speak."

What could she say? "I will pay for it."

The Tom Cat sighed. "Have you the coin?" he asked her. "Have you the coin on you today?"

"I can get it."

He waved an elegant black paw.

"Five days imprisonment," the white Cat ordered.

Horror drenched Livie like cold water. "No—please—"

"Take her away."

The Alsatians approached. Since Livie did not want them to touch her, she moved where bidden to a side door, hearing another name called behind her.

The Cats, even though mechanicals, were bored. They didn't even care that they had sentenced her to—

Jail. Five days.

"Through there," one of the Alsatians barked. She passed through a narrow doorway to a grim corridor that had no relation to the grand chamber behind. Stairs led down to where another pair of Dogs in uniform waited.

"Livie Scrubwoman. Five days jail," barked the Alsatian and Livie was taken into charge.

Three times, while marching down to the cells, her knees threatened to buckle. Fear rolled inside her, along with a measure of anger—outrage—at the unfairness of it. Putting her in jail would not pay for the Ferrets' bauble.

They paused at a desk where her name was taken and her sentence recorded. Then through a heavy metal door and into gloom.

The cells.

It felt cold and dark, and the narrow corridor seemed to stretch out forever. The cells were built of stone with low-slung metal doors set with hatches.

Seemingly at random, the Pitbull who had taken Livie into charge unlocked a door halfway down and ordered Livie inside.

It was dark and felt narrow—for she could see

nothing of the interior—and stank of sweaty human and bodily functions. Livie stumbled forward and the door crashed shut behind her.

Was she alone? No. Someone coughed. She could hear someone else breathing, a harsh rasp.

"Hello?" she said.

No one answered, but she knew they were there—other women as terrorized as she.

Putting out a hand, she felt for the stone wall, cold and clammy. She tripped over someone's legs and fell, landing in straw.

Someone whispered, "Welcome to Hades."

Chapter Nine

"Do they ever feed us?" Livie asked piteously. She had no idea how long she'd been shut in the malodorous, narrow cell. It seemed like an age or perhaps only a few hours.

She still had not seen her companions. With the hatch on the door shut, there was no light and nothing to which her eyes might adjust. She was not even sure how many companions she had.

They did not talk among themselves or speak to her. One of them, obviously quite ill, continued breathing in that painful rasp. Another woman wept steadily.

Never, never had Livie known such despair. Not even at her worst moments out in the world.

At least, when discouraged in the past, she'd been *out in the world.*

How did one measure time here, where nothing happened? That question prompted her to ask about meals, even though she felt far too sick to eat. Something must mark the passage of time.

How would she know when her five days had come and gone? Five days.

An eternity.

Since this was Thursday—would they count today?—that meant she would miss her Sunday with Benton.

*Benton.*

There in the dark, she longed for him with a fervor that went to the bone. She ached for the comfort of him. His arms around her. His mouth at her breast.

What would he think when she didn't meet him on Sunday? Would he go to her room looking for her? Was her room still her room?

She had no way of getting word to him.

"They feed us." A voice came out of the darkness. "Once a day."

"Oh. How many of us are in here? I can't see."

"Five, countin' ye."

Five. Herself, the weeping woman, the rasping woman, whoever spoke to her and—

"Four," said another voice. "I think that one over there is dead."

"What?"

She was trapped in this dark, terrible place with a corpse?

"She hasn't moved or breathed in a while."

"Oh, my God. Won't they carry her out?"

"When they change the buckets, probably."

"What are your names? And how long are your sentences?"

No one answered. They did not want to talk.

Huddled against the wall, Livie drew up her knees and wrapped her arms around them, trying not to think about the presence of a dead woman. Or that if she moved around too much she just might encounter cold flesh.

****

The week passed far too slowly for Benton's liking. His hands healed slowly, subject to such frequent abuse they could do no more than scab over. He had a feeling when they did heal, they would be tougher, with less ability to sense anything. It was the way of their world, wasn't it? Repeated abuse made a person numb.

For all that, he thought about Olivia often and wished he could see her. In an odd way, she accompanied him on his rounds, carried in his mind. He told himself how much better his hands would feel on Sunday when he ran them up her leg. When he cupped her breast. Then nothing else would matter.

Friday came and he went to the meeting located upstairs from the tavern. He became concerned when Olivia was not there, but he told himself she might have been delayed at work, and afraid of getting into any more trouble.

He wanted to stop by her room afterward but dared not be late for his shift.

On Sunday he went to the heroes' statue, where he assumed they would meet, but she did not show up, even though he kicked his heels in the rain for a long while. He went to her room.

Her door stood shut and no one answered his knock until a woman emerged from the next door and whispered at him, "Ye lookin' for Livie?"

"Yes."

The woman's eyes grew large. "I heard she was sent to jail."

What?

"For somethin' that happened at work. Heard it from her Sunday relief woman."

"How long?"

"Eh?"

"To jail for how long?"

"Don't know." The woman shut her door. Benton

94

stood, stunned.

Those damned Ferrets. They'd made a complaint over a trinket no doubt stolen in the first place. Made Olivia's hard life that much harder.

For a moment, rage nearly overwhelmed him. Rage at the unfairness of it and his helplessness. A grown man, he, surviving in a difficult world and performing a dangerous job. Yet he was unable to protect the woman he—well, he didn't dare admit what he felt for Olivia. Lust. Sincere liking. Affection? Yes. It had grown so quickly, so deeply, it still frightened him.

He hated to think of her in a cell. He'd never been sent to jail, but he'd heard plenty of stories, and his very soul flinched from the prospect. To be sure, he couldn't tell which stories were true.

But she would be frightened. Alone. Away from him. Where he could not reach her.

He left her building and went to a tavern for a drink. People said ale never solved anything, but if he didn't have something to steady his nerves, his head just might explode.

The Black Swan was nearest and Danny was behind the bar.

"What's happened to ye?" Danny asked while serving him. "Bad news, man?"

Benton laid his shredded hands on the bar. "The worst. Olivia's been arrested."

Danny peered at him. "Who?"

"Livie. Livie Scrubwoman."

Danny took a step backward. "No! For why?"

"She broke somethin' that belonged to one of her employers."

"Oh, Jesus," Danny said, invoking one of the old

gods. He put an ale in front of Benton.

"It's so damn unfair—" Benton grasped the glass.

"Yes, but keep your voice down." Danny blinked his blue eyes. "The two of ye a couple or somethin', Benny?"

Benton shrugged. "I care about her."

Danny grunted. Hurried away to serve someone else. Benton drank the ale, which seemed to sour in his stomach.

Danny was back before he knew it.

"No wonder she turned me down." Danny took up the conversation as if it had not been interrupted, with the smugness of a born Lothario. "She's with ye."

Benton said savagely, "She's alone now, shut up in that vile pit."

"Yes. For how long?"

"Her neighbor, who told me about it, didn't know. How long could they give her for somethin' like that? Breakin' a bauble."

"With the Cats? Who knows. Ye could look at the lists."

"The what?"

"They always post lists with people's sentences."

"Where?"

"On the wall outside the Council buildin'."

"Thanks." Benton threw back the rest of his ale in one gulp. "I'll go see."

Back out in the rain, it was a long walk to the city's center, up the hill to where the government buildings sat. It being a day of rest for most people, the streets were crowded despite the vile weather. People dodged the carriages of their betters and hoped not to get splashed as conveyances trundled through puddles.

Benton paused at the foot of the hill and regarded the giant complex. Built of stone, with a clock at one corner and turrets at the others, its ornate façade had been darkened by rain and soot. Behind it at the top of the hill rose the Lord High's palace, which looked more like a castle than anything else. The whole of it had a closed appearance like an elderly woman guarding her secrets. How much misery hid there?

And the Lord High, what of him? An ordinary man he had once been, if one possessed of extraordinary talents. One devoid of mercy, who had taken the part of animals and shut himself away from his fellow humans.

Benton trudged up the hill and searched for the wall. It extended to the left of the main doorways where, even though the complex was closed today, two guard Dogs stood.

They did not so much as glance at Benton as he approached the wall, which he could see was tacked liberally with notices, all under glass to protect them from the rain. Others were there before him, staring helplessly.

He could not read well, only what he had picked up, since he'd had no formal education. He did not know which among the many sheets might be the list he sought.

He saw a woman standing before a row of sheets, weeping. Instinct took him there. He puzzled out a heading.

*Sentences.*

His heart jerked in his chest. He stepped closer and tried to puzzle it out letter by letter.

*As decreed by the Council of Cats these are the just and true sentences imposed for human crimes. Take heed.*

He puffed out a breath. The weeping woman departed and he stepped closer.

*Condemned to the cells.*

A list followed. With painful slowness, Benton perused it. So many. Names followed by a term of imprisonment. Everything from days to years. His blood chilled within him.

He found her name at last, spelling that out also. *Livie Scrubwoman. Five days.*

On the face of it, that did not seem so long. Not when others' names were followed by years. Even a few *lifes.*

Life. Spent in some small cell down under this hulking complex. How could even the Cats do that? But this was Olivia. Alone in there.

His rage and frustration made him want to strike the wall, beat on the glass as he saw others must have done, for it was cracked and shattered in places. That would not help Olivia.

How could he help her?

By being here for her, perhaps, when she got out. If that meant he didn't sleep, then he wouldn't sleep.

When would she get out? She'd been sentenced on Thursday. She should be released on Tuesday.

He would be here, waiting.

Till she was freed, though, she must endure. The rest of today. Monday. Whatever portion of Tuesday passed before they released her.

As he moved to turn away, another set of sheets caught his eye. Still lengthier than the jail sentences.

*To the mines for life.*

Name after name after name, all males. All gone, plucked from their lives for crimes real or perceived. For any damn excuse at all.

Never to come back again.

****

After two days passed, Livie's eyes adapted to the darkness enough that she could see her companions as darker shapes that moved, all but for the one stretched out over by the bucket, that didn't. Though they told the Rottweiler who brought their food and the Hound who emptied the bucket that she had died, the corpse was left two more days.

Two days.

It was only when the cell door was opened that Livie got a look at her fellow prisoners, and then the dim light from the hallway seemed so bright it nearly blinded her.

Three women, not counting the dead woman who lay in a little heap with her legs outstretched, her face—mercifully—obscured by a tangle of black hair.

One of the women, she who struggled to breathe and coughed interminably, was aged, at least forty and gray-haired, clothed inadequately in what looked like rags. The woman who wept incessantly had brown hair and did not look much older than Livie, though eventually, when they did get to talking, she said she had three children, now on the outside without her. It was for them she wept.

The last woman—

She bore scars, many of them, a horrific network Livie only glimpsed. A bit older than herself, so she surmised, with fair hair now in a rat's tangle.

It took a while to get them talking. Livie introduced herself and told why she was there. Asked how they would be released.

"Ye'll go on Tuesday, probably in the afternoon,"

said the scarred woman, speaking reluctantly. She gave a spectral laugh. "That's when I'm supposed to get out, though I'll believe it when it happens."

"How long have ye been here?"

"In here and other locations within the dungeons? Years."

*Years.*

"I was held in the deep dungeons for a while. Those cells make this look like luxury. I don't really know how long. Tortured."

Tortured. Those scars.

"Why?" Livie breathed.

"They wanted me to confess. To treason."

"Treason?"

"I used to work as a scribe for the Lord High. They thought I knew secrets and passed them. There were mass arrests to contain the leak."

"Oh."

"The only reason they're releasin' me now is they think my brain's too scrubbed to be a danger."

Livie said nothing. Horrible as it was, her own sentence faded by comparison.

"Gertie there, she's in for stealin' to feed her children. Ammie—the coughin' woman—insulted someone."

"A Ferret," Annie said around a cough.

"I'm in because of a Ferret too."

"I called him an animal. Take my advice, never do that. I got three weeks. My lungs filled up almost at once. The damp."

"And, your name?" Livie asked the first woman.

"I can't remember it." She gave a harsh laugh. "Only that I worked for the Lord High and what they did to me after. They call me Clarkwoman."

"I see. Do ye have anyone on the outside?"

"Lord knows. Not sure what I'll do when—if—I get out on Tuesday."

"Ye'll come home with me." Livie wasn't sure from whence the words originated. They came of their own accord. This woman who had suffered so much could not be turned out with nowhere to go.

"I have—had—a room. If I still have it—"

"That's *kind* of ye." The word came strangely from Clarkwoman's lips, as if she barely remembered its meaning.

"Ye truly don't know your name?"

"Believe me, I remember as little as possible."

Chapter Ten

Benton stood waiting out front of the Council complex on Tuesday afternoon, when people began to emerge.

He had not been to bed but had come here straight from his shift, not knowing when Livie might be released. Hoping she would. The hours had dragged. Many people came and went, but when the pale, ragged individuals began to drift out he straightened to attention from the wall where he'd been half dozing.

They looked so unwell, they had to be prisoners. They paused as if bewildered, blinking at the light of day, appearing lost. There weren't many of them, and Livie came next to last, save for another woman.

"Olivia!" He called to her, and she blinked at him. A hesitant smile came to her face.

Hurrying to her side, he took her in his arms.

"No, I'm filthy, Benton. Filthy."

"I don't care." He drew her in, squeezed her tight, all his frustrated protectiveness coming to the fore. She eased into him, some of her terrible tension ebbing away.

"Are ye all right? Those bastards—"

"I'm all right. Now. What are ye doin' here?"

"Waitin' for ye, of course."

"But ye should be gettin' some sleep."

"No matter. Are ye hungry? We can go to a café—"

"I'm far too dirty. I want to go home. Wash. Change

102

my clothin'. Benton, this is Clarkwoman. She's comin' home with me."

Olivia stepped aside and Benton blinked at the woman who followed her out from the prison. Dressed in rags, she was a sight. Her dark blond hair straggled from her head. Her face was a network of scars from amid which two eyes stared like dark coals. Not as tall as Livie, she was skin and bones, her age impossible to guess.

"Oh, yes?" he said, thrown.

"She's been imprisoned for ages and has nowhere to go."

Had she no family? Benton wondered. But a lot of people had no one. He didn't.

Clarkwoman looked at Benton and swiftly away as if she could bear eye contact with no one. "I will not be fit for the world, not for some time. Livie, if ye want to go off with your young man—"

"We'll get ye settled first," Livie said gently. "Benton, if ye'll escort us home?"

"Certainly."

Thoughts crammed Benton's mind as he shepherded them like two grubby lambs, making way through the crowds and watching out for carriages. A Cat's carriage would run you down as soon as look at you, and some of the Toms cut through the streets at top speeds.

Who was this person? Clarkwoman. What did she mean to Olivia's life? It was good of Olivia to want to help her, but it left an uneasy feeling in the pit of Benton's stomach.

Change usually did, even though in their meetings they swore to work for exactly that—change. This seemed different somehow.

The woman flagged long before they reached Olivia's building, too weak to make the distance. When she drooped and stumbled, Olivia tried to support her but it was clear she herself had little strength to spare. Benton, assisting both of them, found them malodorous. True, the humans in their world did not always smell good. This reached another level.

He had to carry Clarkwoman up the steps to Olivia's third-floor room. He left them to wash and change, saying he would go out for some food.

In truth, he needed to get some distance, to think. To reassess. But his mind refused to process things efficiently.

Oh, Olivia—

**** 

"Your young man could not get away fast enough."

Livie glanced at Clarkwoman with concern. Her guest sat on the edge of the bed, looking like death. A curious assessment to appear in Livie's mind, for though she'd seen a dead person quite recently when the Rottweilers had carried the corpse from their cell, she'd never before beheld a living person who fit the description.

Was Clarkwoman going to survive her release? If she didn't, what would she, Livie, do with the corpse?

"I'm not so sure he's my young man."

Clarkwoman snorted. "Judgin' by the way he looks at ye and the way he embraced ye, I'd say he is."

"That doesn't matter now."

"He might not come back, with me here."

"He'll come back." But Livie did not feel entirely easy about it.

If she'd chased Benton off by extending a hand to

Clarkwoman, that would cause her sorrow. But it would also tell her something important about him, something she needed to know before she got in any deeper.

She eyed her companion, forcing herself to make a fair evaluation. The first real look she'd got at Clarkwoman—other than the glimpses when the cell door opened—had been when they'd emerged from the prison. To say she was shocked would be an understatement. No wonder Benton had fled.

Some of her dark blond hair had fallen out in clumps and been left behind. What remained was tangled. Her eyes, a dark brown, looked stark in her skeletal face. Both her face and hands, which looked like skin stretched over sticks, were hideously scarred, the ridges laid over one another. She looked—barely human.

"That bad, is it?" a corner of Clarkwoman's mouth pulled up in a parody of a rueful smile. "I haven't seen myself in years. I've lost count. No mirrors where I've been, thank God. But your eyes are like mirrors." She hesitated again. "I should leave before your man gets back. Ye don't need me here."

"No. Where would ye go? Out on the streets? Ye know what happens to people who are found on the streets. Ye'd be back in prison before ye knew it. Besides, ye need to recover."

"And it falls to ye to care for me—why?"

"We're friends, aren't we?"

A hardness came to the burning, dark eyes. "If five days together in a cell makes us friends."

"I reckon it does."

"I'm goin' to be a burden, Livie."

"Olivia. Call me Olivia. Shortenin' our names is a way the mechanicals have of demeanin' us, so Benton says."

"Benton's smarter than he looks."

"Ye truly don't remember your name?"

Clarkwoman blinked. "It got blotted out from my mind, like so much else. In fact, they believe they made me forget everythin'—else they'd never have released me." She gave a rather ghastly smile. "I made them believe so. But it's not true."

"Never mind. Maybe as ye recover it will come to ye. There's some water here. It's not fresh but better than what we had in the cell. Hopefully, Benton will bring more from the public fountain when he returns." If he returned. With unsteady hands, Livie poured water into a cup and, discovering Clarkwoman could not hold it for herself, tipped the rim to the woman's lips, which were as filthy as the rest of her.

"We'll use the rest to wash. And then—I don't have much in the way of clothin' but I'll share what I do have with ye. Take these things out for launderin'."

"Mine are fit for nothin' but rags."

It was true.

"Olivia, I can't take what little ye have from ye."

"We'll worry about that later."

Livie locked the door in case Benton did return. Then, very gently, she stripped Clarkwoman down, washed her as she might a child, though she'd certainly never had a child of her own, appalled to discover that the scars extended everywhere on the woman's body. Some of them were deep and showed that various instruments had been employed to pierce, tear, and burn the flesh.

How could anyone endure that? How, and remain sane?

Clarkwoman watched Livie carefully, measuring her reaction to what she saw. Livie did not speak of the damage she witnessed but of other things, murmuring what must seem like nonsense as she sponged the pale, marred skin.

Ending with, "We shall have to choose ye a name, if ye cannot recall yours."

"Do I need a name, beyond Clarkwoman?"

"Indeed. Ye are more than that, surely. Let us come up with somethin' beautiful."

"Even though I am not that?"

Their eyes met for an instant.

"Certainly," Livie said again.

When finished—Clarkwoman's hair had been so tangled, Livie was forced to trim what remained of it— she wrapped Clarkwoman in her shabby dressing gown and stripped down herself for a wash in the now gray water. No need for false modesty, for Clarkwoman sat with her eyes closed, slumped on the bed. Asleep? Passed out? Livie could not tell.

When a soft knock came at the door, Livie's heart leapt. Benton had returned.

He'd brought food and a small flagon of ale.

"How did ye afford all that?" she asked, adding with regret, "Ye'll have gone farther into debt."

"No matter." His gaze flew to the woman on the bed. "Is she all right? Olivia, we have to talk."

"I know. We do." Without hesitation, she moved into his arms. "Thank ye for bein' there when I came out. I don't know what I would have done."

"I want to be here for ye." His lips skimmed over the top of her head and brushed her brow. "When I found out what happened to ye, I was afraid. And angry. So angry."

"Yes."

"Ye must be careful in future. And that means—"

She forestalled what he would say. They spoke in whispers, but she did not want Clarkwoman to hear.

"Benton, I can't abandon her."

"I respect that, I do. But life's enough of a struggle without—"

"She has no one else. She doesn't even remember her name. What they did to her—"

Over Livie's head, Benton shot a look at the woman, now curled on one side.

"Before ye go—for I know ye must get to work—will ye do one more thing for me? Go get a pitcher of water."

"Yes, to be sure."

"I—I suppose I should report for work tomorrow mornin'. I hope I still have a job. If I don't, I can't imagine what I'll do." At least she would not have to face the Ferrets on the morrow.

Benton tipped up her face and gazed into her eyes. "Be careful, please. Ye—ye matter to me. I will go fetch that water."

He went out with the pitcher. Livie did not bother to lock the door this time.

Clarkwoman slept fitfully in the bed. Livie could hear her breathing.

Oh, what had become of her life? She stood at the crux of change, she could feel that.

If she chose poorly, it could cost her everything.

\*\*\*\*

Livie tucked Clarkwoman into bed, dragging her beneath the covers, which cost the last of her strength. Clarkwoman only half roused and mumbled fitfully.

After that, Livie ate ravenously of the food Benton had brought, saving a goodly portion for when her guest might rouse. When it grew dark—while she thought of Benton on his rounds, lighting the lamps—she took a place on the edge of the narrow bed, not touching the woman who lay there, hoping she would not wake beside another corpse.

In truth she slept little and in the morning had trouble rousing Clarkwoman to tell her she must leave for work.

"There's food if ye want it. I shall lock the door. Ye rest."

Clarkwoman rolled hazy eyes at her. Again, when Livie left for work, she wondered what she would find when she returned. A living woman, or something else? And what should she do if Clarkwoman did not survive?

The day's labors near flattened her. She dared not do poorly, skimp in her efforts, or otherwise make a mistake. Her employers, those whom she encountered, did not seem to know she'd been away. So little heed did they pay her, they had apparently not noticed her relief cleaner had left and she had returned.

Just a human, sopping up mud from their homes.

When she got home at the end of the day, Benton was waiting outside. He took her cleaning kit from her and helped her inside. They found Clarkwoman still in the bed, sitting up and looking, if possible, worse than before. The removal of the dirt from her skin had put her scars on stark display, and the clipped head made her a startling sight.

Benton recoiled slightly and remained at the door.

"Will ye be all right, Olivia? I brought more food."

"Ye can't keep doin' that."

He shrugged. "I didn't think ye would feel like goin' out to the shops."

"I am far too weary. So, thank ye." She stretched up and kissed his cheek. "How are your hands?"

"No matter." He pressed them against his trousers. "Will I see ye tomorrow?"

"I do not know. I have to return to the Ferrets' tomorrow." She dreaded it.

"Well," he said darkly, "they have had their satisfaction, haven't they?" He shot a second doubtful look at the woman in the bed. "There's been another meetin' called for Saturday, behind the weaver's. Usual time. Will I see ye there?"

Livie thought about the jail, and the Ferrets, and Clarkwoman's scars. "Yes."

He nodded and went out.

As Livie removed her dripping coat, a weak voice came from the bed, saying, "He does not like me bein' here. I can't say I blame him."

"That's all right."

"If I weren't here, would he stay with ye?"

"We hadn't got to that point yet. Besides, he works nights. We only spent one day—" She broke off.

Clarkwoman gave a weary smile. "And ye'd like another."

"I have to confess…" Livie shivered. "How do ye feel? Did ye eat what I left?"

"Some."

It must have been very little, for a swift perusal showed most of the food Livie had left still remained.

"Will ye try and eat now?" Livie perched on the side of the bed.

Clarkwoman shook her head. "It turns my stomach."

"But ye must gain strength."

Slowly, the dark eyes that held such torment, or the memory of it, met Livie's. "What meetin' was he talkin' about?"

Livie explained about the various groups that made up the resistance, fighting for rights.

"There's a resistance? There wasn't one, back when I—at least, I don't think there was. I've forgotten so much."

"Do ye have any idea how long ye were imprisoned?"

"No. but I was a young girl when I was arrested. No more than seventeen." She spread her skeletal hands. "How old do I look now?"

Impossible to tell. "Why were ye arrested?" They had only touched on this while talking in the cell, but had not gone into detail. There had been a sense of being overheard in the cell, even if they weren't.

Again, the dark eyes found Livie as if plumbing her, measuring her.

"As I told ye, I worked in the Lord High's household, one of many and many to do so. There is an army of helpers and servers to care for that one man. Even then, they rarely see him."

"Did ye ever see him?" Livie asked curiously.

Clarkwoman hesitated. "I did. Eventually. I worked as one of his clerks—or scribes—since I'd been taught while very young to read and write by the Grey Guard who employed my parents. Outside of any school, this was, and I was smart—in those days.

"I helped to copy the Lord High's notes, for he is an inventor, ye understand, and always workin'. A brilliant man..." Clarkwoman seemed to contemplate that fact before she concluded, "if a muddled one, workin' from a skewed reality."

Not at all sure what Clarkwoman meant by that, Livie said nothing.

"I copied mundane things that meant nothin' to me. Lists of supplies or the ingredients for his experiments, I suppose ye would call them. Results of the experiments themselves, both successes and failures."

"Ye remember all that?" Hadn't the torture she'd endured destroyed her memory?

For a third time, Clarkwoman's gaze met Livie's. "I do."

"Oh."

"Copyin' the Lord High's lists and notes required we should be able to read his handwritin', for he made all notations that way. There was a squad of us and some were better than others at transcribin' that scrawl. The others would come to me—"

Clarkwoman stopped abruptly as at a sudden pain.

Livie did not push her. Maybe she did not remember the rest or couldn't bear to recount it.

"It was not a bad life," Clarkwoman said at last. "I ruined it for myself. Olivia, never let your curiosity get the better of ye, for that is exactly what I did, and I have been payin' ever since."

"Oh."

"The squad of us scribes lived in a wing of the palace in a kind of dormitory not far from the Lord High's quarters. One day when I was supposed to be sleeping, for we worked in shifts, I saw his door—that to his workroom, not his sleepin' quarters—stood open. I meant just to peek inside, see perhaps what he was workin' on. For he made all his creatures there and repaired them. It was whispered he was workin' on a crocodile."

Even now, Clarkwoman's eyes grew wide with wonder. "I just wanted to see—" She shook her shorn head. "I should have kept walkin'."

"Ye were caught?"

"I was. But not before seein' some of the wonders within. Great tanks there were, containing components for buildin' his mechanical creatures—fur and pairs of eyes and such. Not the cogs and gears, ye understand, but the preserved livin' bits. There were models, not of a crocodile, I did not see that. But so many others. Parts I did not understand—those were the mechanical parts— scattered on a huge work bench.

"A Cat was lyin' there, a partly disassembled cat in nothin' more than its fur. I could see the inner workin's—the places where he had removed patches of the fur to show the mechanics beneath.

"They are mechanical, Livie," her eyes widened, "for all their cruelty."

"Yes." Nervously and in a whisper, Livie asked, "What happened?"

"There were papers scattered across the work bench. Designs. The original plans for a Cat, they must have been, from which he was workin'. Unimaginably complicated things. Nothing that had ever been transcribed, for these were the notes he kept private."

She paused again, whispered the rest. "Only, see, I could read his writin'."

"Oh," Livie said again in a completely different tone.

"He came in while I stood there. I had just been lookin', I swear to ye as I did to them, over and over again." Clarkwoman's eyes remained dry though tears cracked her voice. "It was just curiosity."

"He did not believe ye?"

"Nay. I was taken away and questioned. They did not believe my answers. I was accused of tryin' to steal his secrets, the most precious of them. I was questioned most—most forcefully. And then more forcefully still.

"They could not release me, thinkin' I knew what I should not, see. And they did not believe I knew not, for those papers had carried delicate secrets indeed."

"Like?"

"Like how to defeat our overlords."

Livie stared at the woman in the bed, who gazed back at her.

"Defeat them!"

"There is a way, Olivia. There is a way."

## Chapter Eleven

"Why didn't they just kill ye?" Livie asked, edging closer to Clarkwoman on the bed, her voice no more than a thread of sound. "If they thought ye had learned somethin' so dangerous."

"I wondered that a thousand times. There were moments I prayed for death. Screamed for it." Clarkwoman looked down at her arms, which rested atop of rough blanket, pale, pale flesh crisscrossed with pink scars and seams. "I do not know, save that some of the mechanicals who questioned me, and they are utterly devoid of mercy as why shouldn't they be, indicated that the Lord High did not countenance outright killin' since so much of it had already taken place durin' the Great Killing.

"Apparently he is devoid of mercy also, for killin' me would have been far, far kinder."

Livie did not know what to say. This wreck of a woman who sat before her should be mad. But she was not mad. She might well have gaps in her memory, but she was rational and making sense.

"Since my questioners did not believe I knew nothin', and since they could not get me to admit to knowin' dangerous secrets, they set out to destroy my mind—if not my body, in the process. They questioned me far past endurance till I was jabberin', and then imprisoned me. Questioned me again just to make sure.

Imprisoned me.

"Only recently was it decided I was so destroyed as to be harmless, and safe to be released."

"Along with me."

"With ye."

"What do they expect ye to do with your life? Released with no place to live and no employment."

"I am convinced they expect me, and the others that are released after long sentences, to crawl away and die."

"But ye will not."

"I am far too stubborn, it seems. There must be a streak of somethin' inside me that will not perish. For if I could have, I would have, there on their table."

Livie wanted to ask what they had done to her—the curious human inside her did. But had she not just heard the price of curiosity? Besides, she was not sure she truly wanted to know.

"Perhaps," she suggested softly, "ye can be rehabituated back into life—"

"I am not sure how. I am used to the seclusion of the cells, silent save for the wailin' and screamin'. Not—not the bustle, ye understand."

Livie nodded. This woman had lived apart from the world for years uncounted.

"But," Clarkwoman said, "there is a hate in me. I don't know if ye comprehend—"

Livie did. She thought of the Ferrets, Pierre and Melia, and the dark feeling arose. "Yes."

"I have very little strength. But I must regain some, if only for that reason." She reached out and clasped Livie's wrist. "Do ye mean to attend the meetin' of which your friend spoke? On Saturday?"

"I don't know." Livie's own head felt scrambled.

And yet, yes, there was injustice that must be addressed. The worst of it lay here before her.

"Ye must go," Clarkwoman insisted.

"Must I?"

"Yes, because I want to go with ye."

"Oh, Clarkwoman, is that a good idea? Ye are so weak."

"I must. Do ye not see? I have to answer the hate within me. For there is nothin' else. It is either that or lie here and die."

"I do see that, yes." Livie thought of her group. "Only we are not exactly the cuttin' edge of the resistance."

"It will have to do. Will ye take me?"

Livie puffed out a breath. "Ye will have to grow stronger. Will ye eat somethin'?"

Clarkwoman closed her eyes. "I will try."

****

There was a feeling out on the streets that night, a sharp edge of something Benton could not identify. Perhaps, he thought as he started his rounds, he'd merely carried his own uneasiness from Livie's room where that woman now lodged. Not that he had anything against Clarkwoman. Only against Livie getting involved in something potentially so dangerous.

But by God, what that woman must have suffered! You could see it on her skin and glimpse it in her eyes. Yes, that was what must be prompting his uneasiness.

Yet it seemed to tremble in the air around him, touching everything. A mild night it was, with only a soft patter of rain, so there were many mechanicals out and about. Cats in their carriages, and large numbers of dandified Foxes out for sport. Animals of all descriptions.

Benton wondered at it. He wondered if the raise in rents had gone through, meaning these mechanicals would split more revenue among themselves. For they lived off not only the misery of those who worked for them but their financial woes also.

It was said the Lord High floated that debt, that he minted the coins on which the world ran and distributed them to the mechanicals, and kept the lists of what humanity owed.

The Debt Rolls, they were called.

But why? If the Lord High were human, why so determinedly keep his fellow humans under?

The elegant and superior beings out on the streets did not seem to see Benton as he went about his rounds. Indeed, he had to step lively more than once to avoid being run down by a carriage or a fast-moving curricle, though the drivers never noticed.

Half way through the night, he met Andy on a street corner and shared a word.

The squat Lightman looked spooked, the way Benton felt.

"Busy tonight, ain't it, Benny?"

"Sure is. Must be the light rain."

Andy gave a shake to his shoulders. "Yes, but there's somethin' in the air, almost like a storm comin'."

They rarely had storms any more. Just the eternal gray cloud cover and unending rain. But yes, Benton knew what Andy meant.

He nodded at a group of passing mechanicals. "D'ye think they know somethin' we don't?"

"God, I hope not." Andy rolled his eyes. "'Cause if they know somethin' we don't, it won't be good for us."

"There's been all that talk of raisin' rents. Maybe it went through."

Andy paled beneath the light of the lamp under which they stood. "We can't afford it. My wife and me—"

"I know." Benton thought of Olivia working so hard, trying to keep her head above water. Would he see her Sunday? Would the presence of Clarkwoman change anything?

Slowly, Andy said, "It does feel like they're celebratin', don't it?"

"Yes. I'd best get back to work before we snag the attention of the Dogs or the Guards."

"Don't want that." Andy made a face. "I doubt I'd last long in the mines."

Benton doubted anyone would.

****

When Olivia emerged from her building to head for work the next morning, she found Benton waiting. She blinked at him in surprised delight.

"Thought ye might like me to walk ye to work," he told her. "I just finished my rounds and can head for home after." He hesitated. "I knew ye'd be nervous, goin' back."

She was. The ball of dread in her stomach, a product of having to face the Ferrets today, just kept getting bigger. Worse, they were her last assignment of the day, so she'd have to keep dreading the encounter all day long.

"What if they're not satisfied with my imprisonment, the Ferrets? What if they try to cause me more trouble?"

"They won't. The debt's been paid. That's how their

119

world works."

He took her bucket from her and carried it in addition to his own pack, slung on his back. "How is your guest doin'?"

"A little better. We talked some." Livie shivered. "Benton, ye wouldn't believe what she's been through, what they've done to her."

He grunted. "I can tell some, by lookin' at her."

"I have to help her. There's no one else."

Benton said nothing. She stopped walking and turned to face him. "This won't change anythin' between us, will it? Clarkwoman bein' here, I mean. I still want to see ye on Sunday." She threw her heart into it. "I ache to be with ye."

Something in his eyes eased. "Then we'll go to my room."

"And—and make love?"

"If that's what ye want."

"Benton, I didn't have a chance to tell ye, with Clarkwoman there and all. But—in the jail, in that cell— I clung to ye. To the idea of ye, if ye know what I mean."

"I do. I've been clingin' to ye as well."

"I could hardly bear missin' our Sunday together, and—and—" To her dismay, her eyes filled with tears.

Gently, he touched her hair. "Was it very terrible, Olivia?"

"Awful. It stank and they barely fed us and one of the women had died—they didn't take her body away for days."

"Oh, God."

"And the dark—it was so, so dark. I felt like I breathed that dark. There only a bucket for—for needs."

"Don't dwell on it, love. Don't, now." He drew her into his arms.

*Love.*

Did he, could he love her? Did she love him? Could there be anything more foolish in their world than falling in love?

"We'll be together Sunday," he murmured. "We'll make it all better."

She kissed him. Right out there on the street, she did.

Passersby might have stared, human and mechanical alike. She barely cared. Such comfort lay in the kiss as a means of communication that went beyond words.

"Come along," he said then. "I don't want ye to be late."

"No." God forbid she make another blunder.

Her first three assignments went as usual. Either she did not see her employers, only the House Mice, or they acted as if they'd not noticed she'd been gone.

Another lesson, she thought as she scrubbed mud from the floor. One of the many she seemed meant to learn.

Her stomach turned sick as she approached the Ferrets' house and was admitted by their House Mouse. *Please do not let the Ferrets be home.*

Pierre was not—busy pursuing his profession, no doubt. But Melia came out of their parlor to watch Livie at her work, a sharp look in her small, dark eyes. As if she did not trust Livie as far as she could toss her.

Livie felt exhausted by then, her five days of deprivation having debilitated her, but she dared not move wrong.

Melia did not speak, nor did Livie. She crawled across the foyer floor, scrubbing up mud, and made sure to skirt any furniture there, so she would not accidentally bump into it. The table she'd bumped last time had a new bauble on it, a tall, blue urn.

"I see you have learned your lesson," Melia said in her squeaky mechanical voice when Livie finished. "Now get upstairs and dust those chambers."

Resentment rose up inside Livie as she scrambled to her feet, so strong it nearly chased the exhaustion. She had learned a lesson. That was all her five days of suffering meant to these heartless mechanicals.

She had to remember, despite their fur and claws and bright eyes, they were no more than machines. The true animals of the past were no more.

She barely had the strength to walk home, hauling her bucket. The three flights of stairs stole what little she had left, and she reached her door sagging.

Had Clarkwoman been all right while she was gone? What would Livie find when she opened the door? What if the woman had died in the bed sometime during the long day?

Before Livie could juggle the bucket and unlock the door, her neighbor, Cassie, stuck her head out from her own room. "Oh, Livie, it's ye." She spoke in a loud whisper. "Have ye heard?"

"Heard? Nay, what?" Livie shook her head. She just wanted to go inside.

"There's been a new decree come down from the Lord High. Late yesterday afternoon it was. It's all over the street and in the broadsheets too, the ones that go out to the mechanicals."

"What kind of decree?"

Cassie seemed to shrink where she stood. "The mechanicals now have the right to eliminate us if they deem it necessary. Without a trial or a hearing. So long as they report it afterward to a Cat or a Dog and turn the body over for—er—disposal."

"What?" Livie repeated though she'd heard every word. "But, how can that be?" She'd thought the Lord High avoided killing, after so many had been lost. Hence Clarkwoman's torture and eventual release. "There's no justice—"

"It's their justice."

"But, why? Why would the Lord High hand down such a dangerous order?" Why, for that matter would he betray his fellow humans?

He was human, so they said. But, to be sure, he'd already betrayed them.

Cassie whispered, "They're sayin' on the street it was prompted by an incident, but I don't know what that incident was. I was at work all day." Like Livie, Cassie scrubbed.

The Ferrets could kill her out of hand next time she broke something. No hearing before the Council of Cats. No time in jail. Just a summary death.

Terrifying.

With shaking fingers, Livie fitted the key into the lock and went in.

For one terrible moment, she thought Clarkwoman was dead. She lay unmoving on the narrow cot, the blanket drawn up and head turned on the pillow, eyes closed.

Livie caught her breath. But when she shut the door and set down her bucket, Clarkwoman moved feebly.

"Olivia?"

"It's me."

"What time is it?"

"The end of my shifts."

"I've slept the day away." Clarkwoman's dark, smoldering gaze met Livie's. "What is it? Ye look upset."

"It's been a—a long day. And I just heard from my neighbor there's been a decree."

She stumbled to the foot of the bed and collapsed there, tears swamping her. They were tears of terror and exhaustion and dread so deep she could not express it other than by weeping.

Clarkwoman pulled herself up in the bed, but did not ask questions. She let Livie cry until the tears ran out and Livie was able to choke out words relating what Cassie had told her.

"If it's true," she concluded, "the mechanicals have just been given tremendous power over us—beyond what they already had. Without any oversight or hope of justice."

Emotions burned in Clarkwoman's eyes and in her scarred face. "Was there any real justice, anyway? Was there ever a hearin' before Council that went in favor of a human?"

"Maybe not. But grantin' mechanicals the right to kill us out of hand—"

"As we used to do to them, long ago." Clarkwoman seemed to muse. "Cows and pigs slaughtered in their thousands for meat. Dogs and Cats put to death summarily in what were called *shelters*. Game animals shot. It was no game for them, was it? Some people even shot their own pets, if they misbehaved."

"Are ye sayin' this new decree is fair? How can ye, after what they did to ye?"

"I'm not sayin' it's fair. I'm tellin' ye what they will

claim—that humans were never fair either. It's the way they think."

"But, the Lord High! He's human, isn't he? How can he countenance this?"

"He's a different sort of human. One who, I suspect, hates and scorns his own kind."

"It terrifies me."

Clarkwoman gazed at her a long time. At last she said, "This meetin' of the resistance—it is when?"

"Saturday, late afternoon."

"I will attend."

"But—" Livie eyed her companion while trying not to be obvious about it. "I'm not sure—"

"I will attend. It should be quite the interestin' meetin', don't ye think? In light of all this."

Livie supposed it would.

Chapter Twelve

Benton heard the news as soon as his feet hit the cobbles that night. No less than three of his fellow Lightmen stepped up and told him. And he found out exactly why so many mechanicals had been out amid an air of celebration the previous night.

They had indeed been celebrating.

Still and all, he could scarcely believe it. For all the unbalance of power in their world, the Lord High—and his mechanicals—had at least pretended to respect a system of justice, one that echoed what had existed in their world before the Great Killing.

To wipe that out in essence by granting mechanicals the right to summarily put to death any human they deemed deserved it—

"The decree says 'humanely,' " shared Andy, when Benton met him. "We are to be put to the death humanely. Whatever that means. I've read it. Copies of the decree are tacked up all over the City, the nearest at the old church on Warden Street."

Benton had gone by to look at it in lieu of taking his break. He and the other lamplighters no longer met on a corner to talk and share a nip. They would henceforth not dare.

It was raining hard and he couldn't get near the church door, for there was a line of men and women there. The faces of those coming away told him much of what he needed to know. As did the cries of others around him.

"Is it there?"

"Is it true?"

He dared not wait and see for himself. He had to return to his route.

There were still more mechanicals out on the streets despite the heavy rain, and they again wore an air of celebration—made darker now that Benton knew the reason for it.

They celebrated their right to kill him and his kind, at their choosing. Men. Women. Children, if they found them.

He thought of Olivia. Precious to him, she was. He was not certain what his feelings for her meant, colored as they were by a frustrated desire to protect.

The thought that she could be hauled up like vermin and—well, killed on her job, he supposed. For any cause a mechanical declared justified.

Mechanicals could think. They could not feel. They could not empathize.

Of course, people—who could empathize—often did not. This decree would spark anger. Trouble would ensue.

He could feel it in his bones.

After his shift he went to the tavern, where chaos reigned. Everyone spoke at the same time, some claiming the decree could not be true, others declaring they'd read it with their own eyes. Many, who could not read at all, stood frustrated. Fear and anger were alive in the room.

Benton did not even attempt to get a drink. He just stood among the crowd and listened.

"We won't stand for it!"

"They can't treat us this way."

"They might own our souls for debt, but to give them cold metal bastards the right to kill us—"

"Death to the Lord High!"

The cry brought a hushed silence. They might be angry, yes, but such words were treason and might earn execution at any time. And there were always mechanical ears nearby.

"Careful, man!" cried someone else in a hoarse whisper. "D'ye want to condemn us all?"

And there lay the fear, now heightened.

As the impromptu meeting continued, Benton did learn what had prompted the new decree, for they discussed that also.

An incident had occurred way over in Brill Street, the other side of the City. Apparently a mob of men, two nights before last, attacked a squad of Foxes out carousing, had used clubs and tools on them, and beaten them so badly they could not be repaired.

Some of the men had been captured by Dogs on patrol nearby, and members of the Grey Guard. Others had got away.

Those caught were already dead.

Benton could understand the impulse that had moved those men. The desire to use what tools came to hand and attack. Maim. Not a man gathered there in the tavern but comprehended it.

Those bands of Foxes were insufferable, walking around town in their finery like so many dandies, their sharp faces superior. And anything mechanical could be beaten into mere components, springs, cogs, and gears.

But look what it had earned them!

The discussion went long and nothing was decided before Benton went home to bed. What could be decided, when they had no power?

He wondered if Olivia had heard. Wondered if she was all right. When he lay down on his bed he wished she were there with him.

He got some sleep and rose to attend the meeting at the weavers'. He definitely wanted to be there even though such gatherings had just become a thousand times more dangerous.

He decided to swing by Olivia's building on the way. There was an increased police presence on the street, Rottweilers, Dobermans, and Shepherds. And the Alsatians were out, ever watchful. Just waiting for someone to make a misstep.

He found Olivia leaving her building to attend the meeting. With Clarkwoman.

The woman looked milk-white beneath her scars and appeared so weak she could barely stand. Instinct made Benton step forward to the stoop, blocking their way.

"What are ye doin'?" he asked, his fear making him sound harsher than he intended.

"Goin' to the meetin'. Have ye heard—"

"Yes. I just came from the tavern."

"Benton, what are we to do?"

He wasn't sure they could do anything. Fear flickered within him like candle wicks raked by a cold wind.

He fixed his gaze on Clarkwoman. "Is it a good idea for ye to be out of that room?"

"I mean to attend the meetin'." Even her lips were pale. But her eyes glowed like wicks inside her.

129

"Listen, why don't ye wait till ye're stronger? There are police all over. And ye don't want to draw any attention."

Her lips twisted. "Keep our heads down and hope we escape notice, is that it? But that doesn't always work. Especially now."

"I hear ye. But please, go back inside for now."

"I'm sorry to disappoint ye, Benton, but I will not."

"She's comin', Benton." Olivia raised her chin. "I think she's earned the right, don't ye?"

They had no rights. None. But Benton did not say so. And when Clarkwoman faltered and nearly collapsed less than half the distance to the weavers' establishment, he swung her up in his arms and carried her the rest of the way.

People stared. Of course they did; the three of them made quite the sight.

The Dogs on patrol stared also, which bothered Benton far more.

They did not want to lead anyone to the illicit meeting.

That being so, he stopped with them first at a nearby café and asked for a way out the back and there, through an alley, to the rear of the weavers'.

A humble place, this—not the kind of shop that made cloth for the gloriously clad mechanicals but for humans. The hand looms stood deserted now and the place had a spooky feel, with the rain crashing outside and a larger number of humans than usual in attendance.

The decree had raised emotions, all right. Barely had Billy Spade called the meeting to order than people began to speak, condemning the decree, decrying how dangerous it was, and asking how they might get the

Lord High to rescind it.

"A delegation to him, perhaps?" someone suggested with terror in her eyes. "Or a letter?"

"Would he care?" A man tossed out. "I am no longer sure he is human."

"He is a genius," said another woman. "They think differently."

All the while, people in the roughly formed circle had been stealing looks at Clarkwoman. No question why. She might well have been a living corpse, and had they not been so distracted by their outrage, they might have questioned her presence.

When she did speak at last, when all the fears and arguments and pleas had begun to run down, she immediately captured their attention.

"I have personal knowledge of the Lord High. Can anyone else here say so?"

Silence fell. To be sure, no one could. They stared at her and stole looks at one another.

Clarkwoman's voice sounded rusty and raw. "I once worked for him. Saw him frequently. I no longer remember what my name was back then. Ye can see what was done to me, that made me forget."

They could see. It became so quiet, the rain outside sounded doubly loud.

"He is a genius, yes, as ye've said. A recluse who detests his fellow men. I suspect they must have treated him badly in the past, before the Great Killing. His favored companions then may have been animals.

"Either way, I do not believe any appeal for mercy or justice will move him. Ye must focus on more direct and possibly more violent means."

\*\*\*\*

"She is mad," Benton said. "I hope ye realize that. I hope everyone back in that meetin' realizes it. Because what she suggests is so dangerous—"

They stood outside the closed door of Olivia's room speaking in whispers. Benton had already carried Clarkwoman in and put her on the bed. Now he wanted to make sure Olivia saw reason.

"I do not believe she is mad, not entirely." Olivia raised her chin.

Benton lowered his voice still farther. "Look at her. Anyone can see her body's shattered, and her mind also. Think about it, Olivia. Would they have released her if they weren't certain of that?"

Olivia considered the point, her gaze clinging to his. "I suppose not."

He puffed a breath between his lips and cradled her shoulders in his hands. "God knows, I want there to be hope. Somethin' we can do about this damned decree. I don't think it rests on her."

"Hope keeps goin' away bit by bit, it does. Bein' in jail taught me that. Any of us can just be taken away at any time. What are we to do about the decree? Benton, the Ferrets could kill me next time I step wrong, with no repercussions."

"I know, love. I know." He tightened his fingers on her shoulders, aching to protect her. "But for her to suggest violence—"

Especially knowing, as Clarkwoman did, what the consequences could be.

"Ye're right, we have to be careful."

"Yes."

"That doesn't mean we can give up."

Benton supposed it didn't. Still, a kind of terror

simmered inside him—for Olivia, if not himself. It was cowardly to wish some other arm of the resistance would step up, not theirs. But he ached to protect her any way he could.

"Just be cautious," he begged her. "If Clarkwoman's head is not right, don't let her talk ye into anythin'. Promise?"

"I promise."

He bent toward her. "I'll still see ye tomorrow?" He ached for that also, in a manner that fair astonished him. For a man who'd gone so long without sexual contact, he had quite an appetite.

Her eyes brightened and she nodded. "Yes. Oh, yes."

"We can spend the day together. All day."

She nodded again. "Shall I meet ye at the statue?"

"Yes. I'll take ye to my room."

"I hope Clarkwoman will be all right alone so long. I will leave her some food and water. She sleeps most the time anyway."

Benton kissed her because he did not want her thinking of Clarkwoman. Only of him. He wanted to lose himself in the world of her. Of them.

"Right. I'm off to work."

"Won't ye need to sleep tomorrow?" she asked shyly.

"I need ye far more than sleep." He kissed her again, the kind of kiss meant to keep him warm the rest of the night.

****

When Livie slipped into the room, Clarkwoman met her with a serious gaze. Livie wondered how much of her conversation with Benton the woman had heard through

133

the door. Not much, surely.

"Ye must be exhausted," Livie said, and took off her coat.

"No one believed me," Clarkwoman said. "They all think me mad, don't they? Just like your friend."

So she had listened through the door.

"I doubt they know what to think, Clarkwoman. They can see your condition. And it's doubly dangerous now to talk of violence."

Clarkwoman waved one skeletal hand. "It's no different than it was, only its out in the open now. A stated threat rather than a hidden one. Do ye truly think the Lord High couldn't have had me killed any time he chose rather than leavin' me there with the torturers?"

Livie went and sat on the bed. "Maybe. But now— the difference is, it won't require his order. Any mechanical can decide we're too loud, too disobedient, too troublesome—and kill us on the spot."

"Men die every day in the mines. It just happens more slowly."

"True. And bein' sent there is the equivalent of bein' sentenced to a slow execution. But now we have hundreds of potential executioners. All my employers. The Dogs on the street. The Grey Guard. We live at the whims of the Foxes and God knows how fickle they are."

Clarkwoman turned her face away. "Ye don't believe me either. That I know a way to defeat them all."

"Do ye? Somethin' ye held on to through all they did to destroy your mind?"

"Yes."

Livie drew a breath. She did not want to admit outright that she doubted her companion. Besides, there was a part of her that did believe.

She changed the subject. "I'm plannin' to spend tomorrow with Benton. Will ye be all right on your own here?"

"To be sure, I've spent days in far worse places than this." She swung back to face Livie. "Have your day with your young man while ye can."

"I mean to. But—"

"Olivia, I have all I need." A curious smile twisted Clarkwoman's scarred lips. "All, perhaps, but revenge."

A chill chased its way up Livie's spine. But no, she refused to let even her disquiet ruin the day ahead.

Chapter Thirteen

Rain fell hard when they met at the heroes' statue, so they did not linger but moved off to Benton's room straight away. It proved, if anything, even more cramped than Livie's tiny space. He possessed only a bed, a few hooks on the wall, and a spot in the corner for his kit. It seemed still smaller with his large form and Livie's inside. But it did possess a narrow window against which the rain spattered and dripped.

They lost no time in shedding their wet clothes and then kissed, skin to skin. The magic of it, the bliss of being with this man, overtook Livie immediately and drove all other thoughts from her head.

She knew what to expect, or thought she did, when they reached the bed. He worshipped her with his lips, from head to toe, making her nipples prick in the cool air. When he latched on to a breast, she believed there was nothing more than this to be found in the world. Just his mouth and big hands on her. No fear. No worry.

When she could bear the sharp ache of it no longer, she urged his mouth down between her thighs which he parted gently, before pleasuring her to climax. After, he crawled his way back up her body and she gazed into his eyes.

"Let me, Benton. Let me drink from ye now." He was hard against her, hot and heavy.

"Love." He nuzzled her neck. "I want that, sure. I

want somethin' else more."

Something else?

She blinked at him hazily. No lights illuminated the room but a gray thread of daylight came in the fogged window. By it she could see that his eyes, close up, were definitely not mud-colored but amber, gold, and green mixed with brown.

"I want to be inside ye, Olivia."

"But ye said—" Dangerous. She could conceive his child, if he released inside her.

Their whole world was dangerous.

"Yes."

He kissed her, his tongue penetrating in a parody of what she instinctively knew would happen below. Already, she belonged to him in body and possibly soul. Could she deny him anything?

Still gently, he bent her legs up and parted them. Never, never in the whole of her life had she been so open to anyone as to this man. This man she—

With one swift demanding stroke, he took her and bedded himself inside. He was big, yes, but his lavish blandishments had prepared her and, save for a pinch of pain and a catch in her breath, she accepted him. Accepted and gloried in the sensation. A part of him inside her. Hers, entirely.

"Oh," she said. "Oh!"

He moved very gently at first, and his movement called up her own, tentative, and utterly instinctive. She tilted her body to meet the thrust of his and a wildness came into her head, so she heeded nothing save how they fitted together, how they rocked together. And the pleasure she'd known only moments before built still more strongly, to a crescendo that outshone anything that came before.

When he released himself inside her, her body fluttered and convulsed, drew in more deeply what he gave. Time suspended, their bodies joined above and below, his heart hammering against her as if it drove her blood as well as his own.

He made to withdraw and she belayed him, curling her legs around his large body and holding him in. He stopped kissing her and once more they gazed into one another's eyes.

"Stay. Please."

He did, filling her. He rested on his forearms there in the bed so he wouldn't crush her, and continued gazing at her in a manner that said what words never could.

It was she who sought for words. "We are no longer two people," she whispered, "but one."

He smiled.

"Before—that was good. I still want to drink ye, Benton. I've been cravin' the taste of ye. But this, oh, this—"

He brushed his lips over hers softly. So gentle for such a big man, except for that first thrust that had claimed her soul.

"It's a part of bein' human, isn't it?" she asked, all her words his, as was the rest of her. "Our bodies fittin' this way."

"If I stay inside ye, I'm goin' to grow hard again."

"Oh, good."

He laughed, a deep rumble that rose from his chest and set her skin to tingling. So rare a sound was it, it felt like a gift or a prize.

"Do that," she urged, and kissed him, and with very

little persuasion they did it all over again.

\*\*\*\*

"I like your body," Livie told Benton sometime later when, temporarily spent, they lay in one another's arms. Benton had no doubt whatever that the condition was merely temporary.

"Do ye?" he purred.

"Umm-hmm." With artless possession, she caressed him. "I like ye when ye're standin' and when ye go soft. I like the hair on your chest and down below. I like the feel of it on my tongue. I like your broad chest. How big ye are. I love the taste of ye."

"Ah." He nuzzled her neck. "So I've noticed."

Time had gone away since they fell onto his bed together, slipped entirely from his grasp. He had no idea if it were morning or afternoon. Light still trickled in through the little window. It continued to rain. Livie denied him nothing of herself, anywhere he wanted to touch or to taste.

Lazily, he caressed her breast, the nipple puffed and swollen from his previous ministrations. She had what he considered absolutely perfect breasts. Just the right size, full and buoyant.

She moaned at his touch and tugged his head down to her bosom so he could do nothing but latch on. She caressed his head as he suckled and the strong magic stole through him again.

Wonderful. Terrifying. How could he ever live without this woman?

He migrated from one breast to the other and felt himself rise.

She laughed, a doting sound. "I thought ye said ye must rest a while?"

Seemed he'd been mistaken.

She would be sore tomorrow. They both would. But when she spread herself beneath him, he could do nothing but enter her.

Another one of those long joinings when she held him inside her. The greatest pleasure Benton had ever known.

He wanted to tell her he loved her. To get on his knees and beg her to marry him, to belong to him and only to him forever. The impulse seemed as strong as all the others at work between them.

He reminded himself that they were caught up in wonder, in passion. She'd been with no other man. How could she know it was only Benton she wanted, with his great clumsy body and weighty debt?

So he said nothing, not even when at last she released him and cuddled up beside him. captured his hands one after the other and examined the palms.

"These aren't healin' very well, are they?"

"They have very little chance for it when I'm usin' them to climb every night."

She caressed his palms one by one with a gentle forefinger and laid them to her breasts. "I wish I could heal ye."

"I wish I could protect ye."

An impossibility.

"Let's sleep a while. And then—"

"And then."

She dozed against him while he lay with his eyes wide and cradled her, unable to find sleep. His thoughts were strained even if, for the moment, his body seemed compliant. If he could have his choice, he would ask no more from life than this. Olivia in his arms, the right to be with her as often as possible. Would their world permit?

When she woke, he asked if she was hungry. Only for him, she answered and proved it. Then she told him, "I want to stay here all night. Is that all right with ye?"

"It is. What about your guest?"

"I'll stop by on my way to work to get my bucket and check on her."

\*\*\*\*

Come morning, they dressed in the cold, damp light coming through the window and Livie made the bed, not liking to see it untidy. She hated the very idea of parting from Benton but now, more than ever, they dared not step out of line.

"Olivia," he said when they stood outside his door, "why don't ye move in with me?"

Surprise lifted her gaze to his face. "Yes? But I have my room."

"Ye can keep it. Leave it to Clarkwoman for now. Ye don't need to tell anyone ye've moved out."

"Are ye sure?" She examined his expression, wondering what had prompted the offer. Was it merely passion speaking? They had shared much and much on the two occasions they'd been together. Maybe, being a man, he just wanted more of the same.

Being a woman, perhaps she did also. Yet her heart was already involved. She knew that as clearly as she felt the remnants of his touch on her skin. A soreness here. A tender abrasion there. Dared she risk her heart?

Dared she do anything else?

"Ye're jumpin' at this pretty quick," she told him. "Maybe ye should think about it."

"Maybe ye need to think before ye give me your

answer." He seized her around the waist and drew her up against him with the masterful possessiveness born during their hours together. "I'm certain."

"Let me take the prospect to Clarkwoman. She needs a lot of help and might not like the prospect of bein' alone."

He did not appreciate that. Livie could see the protest in his eyes. But he nodded and did not argue it.

She leaned up and kissed him slowly, luxuriously. Better than breakfast or a drink after going without. "I'll talk to her tonight. No time now, I must run."

She barely focused on her work that day—the usual Monday run-through—though she did remember to keep her ears peeled for any talk about the decree on the part of her employers. There was none. All four houses were quiet, even the mud seeming less horrendous. Did the House Mice she encountered eye her more sharply than usual? Looking for an excuse, perhaps, to condemn her to death? No, likely just her imagination.

Exhaustion pulled at her as she hurried home through the eternal rain. She'd not had enough sleep last night, being concerned with other pursuits, and now the lack caught up with her.

She stared blearily at the mechanicals that passed her on the street, the Cats in their grand carriages, the bands of well-dressed Foxes and Badgers. Running on steam, driven by their cogs and gears, they did not know what it felt to be weary. To fall sick. To desire. All these were human things.

As, so they would say, was cruelty.

Yes, humans had been cruel in the past to the creatures with whom they shared the world. Some might say humans deserved their current predicament. Clearly, the Lord High thought so. Yet something had been lost also in the transformation of flesh-and-blood animals to metal-and-steam.

Had there not in the past been good and loving relationships between humans and companion animals? Had not shepherds taken good care of their flocks and some farmers done right by their stock?

Livie, of course, could not remember these times, but she'd heard the stories.

Once there had been love as well as cruelty.

Now, these mechanicals splashed by her on her weary way as if she did not exist. As if they would not spit on her, if able. They were incapable of love.

She hurried to her building and up to her room, thinking how curious it was she'd never before truly considered that part of it. The love. Did it only enter her mind now because she grew feelings for Benton?

Did she love him?

She didn't know. There were strong feelings, tender ones. But she couldn't say she understood love.

She found Clarkwoman asleep, still catching up on the rest she'd missed, but the woman roused when Livie came in and set down her bucket.

"Oh, Olivia, what time is it?"

"Half past six."

"Are ye goin' back out for a meetin'?"

"Not tonight. How do ye feel?"

"To tell ye the truth, I'm not sure." Clarkwoman looked at Livie uncertainly. "I do not know where the day has gone."

"The sleep can only do ye good," Livie told her, ignoring the fact that Clarkwoman did not look any better. Still bone-thin and white as her pillow. "Did ye take anythin' to eat today?"

"I scarcely rose from the bed."

"I'll make us somethin'."

Livie removed her sopping coat and bustled around, dividing bread and cheese. She sat on the end of the bed and they shared the portions.

"Ye'd best eat that, all of it."

Livie was ravenous. The work of the day on top of the previous day and night's exertions had famished her.

Another part of being human.

Clarkwoman watched her with burning, dark eyes and only nibbled at her food. A fire existed, so Livie could see, within the woman's frail form. Had it been that fire that refused to go out even under torture?

"I've been havin' dreams," Clarkwoman announced. "When I sleep. Only I can't really tell if they're dreams or memories."

Livie stopped eating to stare.

"I see him. the Lord High. And I see myself at work copyin' his notes, before—before—"

"Perhaps ye should not think about it." Livie could only imagine the other, terrible memories that could follow.

"But some of the memories are valuable."

"Yes, so ye said. A way of defeatin' our oppressors."

She must have disguised any true memories, or the Cats and the Grey Guards never would have let her leave custody. Had she buried them beneath a kind of madness? Was Clarkwoman mad?

"I feel," Clarkwoman played with her hunk of bread, "I must sort the dreams from the memories. I do not want to stay this way. I dare not."

"How can I help?"

"Ye are already givin' me so much help, with a safe roof over my head." Clarkwoman lifted her chin. "I don't doubt when the authorities released me they believed I would die in the street."

Livie didn't doubt it either.

"But ye were there—here—to help me. It was fate that we met in that cell."

Perhaps.

"I will never, ever be the woman—the girl, actually—I once was. But I must fight to be more than *this*."

Livie nodded.

"To that end, I want to choose a new name since I cannot, for the best of me, remember my old one. It's odd—I can almost, almost catch it. The sound of the questioners hollerin' my name at me as they applied the irons or the clips or the blades. But—" she shook her head, "it's gone."

"I think choosin' a new name would be a fine thing." A step back, maybe, from the brink. "What d'ye fancy?"

"I have been thinkin' about that all day. I want it to be somethin' bright. Victorious."

As was deserved, Livie acknowledged.

"I'm thinkin'—Gloria."

"I like that." Livie could not help but smile.

The woman in the bed nodded slowly. "And I want ye to take me to all the meetin's. I want to participate in them. To make a difference."

"All right. But ye must be careful. Take it slowly."

"I will."

"Listen, Gloria, Benton has asked me to move in with him."

"Has he?"

"Yes."

"And what do ye want?"

"I—I think I want to be with him."

"Then that is what ye must do."

"Yes, but it's risky, isn't it? I've never before risked my heart."

"D'ye trust him?"

"Yes." That was among the foremost of what she felt for Benton. That had allowed her to give him her body. Open herself the way she had, to him.

"Do ye think he would hurt ye?"

"No, I don't, not on purpose, anyway. But what if he's deceived in his feelin's for me? It's happened so quickly. I went from just glimpsin' him at the meetin's to—to—"

"Yes."

"It's so easy, in our world, to get hurt."

"That is true."

"Then again, there's so little that's joyful in our world. I'd be mistaken in forgoin' what I've found."

"Is that how he makes ye feel? Joyful?"

"When I'm—er—with him, yes. I've never felt anythin' to match it."

"Then I believe it will be wise to take up his offer. I can move out of here, find another place."

"No. Gloria, I'll keep the room. If I move in with Benton, it will be yours."

Gloria's lips trembled. "I can't let ye do that. Ye pay for the rent, d'ye not?"

"Yes, and will continue to do so. So long as I stop by here often, and I will do, to check on ye, no one need know the difference. If I keep some of my things here

146

and we tell no one, it should be fine."

"Ye are a good woman. A generous and gracious one. I wish I could give somethin' back to ye."

"Just grow strong and continue to heal. Do ye think the Council will eventually assign ye a job?"

"I do not know. If they consider me mad—"

And they wanted her to die on the street. But that would not happen.

"Ye have offered me the gift of security," Gloria said. "I will find a way to repay ye, so I do swear."

Chapter Fourteen

The first execution performed under the new decree came scarcely a week later. Word of it was passed on the street from mouth to ear, from human to human. Later, it was splashed across the broadsheets that were put out by the Grand Council.

Human Officially Removed for Theft.

*Removed.* So that was the term by which they meant to call it.

Livie was living with Benton by then and they'd fallen into the habit of meeting at his room after her day scrubbing ended and before his shift began. They would share a few words, a few kisses before he took up his kit and went off into the gathering dark, and she left her bucket and returned to visit Gloria.

It wasn't much to live on but enough, and Sunday promised to make up for it.

This day, Olivia was waiting for him when he came in and she hurriedly asked, "Did ye hear?"

"Yes. It's all over the City. And look." He brandished the broadsheet he'd brought. They perched on the edge of the bed and perused it with some difficulty, spelling out the words.

"It was a woman," Livie breathed.

"Yes. A Bathwoman." One of the poor creatures who worked in a public bathhouse.

"Killed for theft."

"What did she steal?"

"It says here, a heel of bread. From one of her human customers."

"A human? Surely one of us wouldn't turn another in."

"No. But—" Benton stared into the air, "don't ye see? That makes it better for them. The transgression wasn't against a mechanical. They can say it was unprejudiced. Justice." He swallowed hard. "They've been waitin' for just such an opportunity."

Not long, they hadn't.

"It says here she stole the food—" Livie faltered, "—for her children."

"Yes. Took the bread from her customer's coat pocket and put it in her apron. When the man made an outcry—for he saw her do it—the Frogs runnin' the house stepped in. The Grey Guard was called. The sentence was imposed at the insistence of the Frog who said he didn't want any trouble on his premises."

"No trouble—like killin' a woman?" Olivia's eyes filled with tears so she could barely read the newsprint. "It says when they dragged her outside and into the street, she wept. Offered to give the bread back. Said her children were starvin'. Just before they killed her—she cried out, askin' what would happen to them."

Benton lowered the sheet.

"What will happen to them?" Livie asked.

"God knows."

"I'm not sure I believe there is a God. There can't be, if things like this can happen."

Benton sighed. "I must get to work. I dare not be late."

"No. No, ye cannot be late." Livie's heart spasmed

with fear, and when he got to his feet she rose too, and laid hold of the front of his coat. "Ye'll be careful? Careful not to step wrong. I really don't know what I'd do if—" She'd taken such pains for so long, not to risk her heart. Now he held it in his keeping.

"Yes. And ye. Have a care if ye go and see Gloria." He had accepted the name readily.

They kissed, and it tasted of desperation.

****

Three more executions by decree—or Removals as the mechanicals insisted on calling them—swiftly followed. All three arose in the wake of the riots and protests that followed Callie Bathwoman's death. She was far more famous in death than she had been in life.

Humans—males for the most part—took to the streets damaging anything that belonged to mechanicals. Windows of the fine houses were smashed. Rocks were thrown at carriages. The members of the Grey Guard were harassed.

When a group of humans attacked a lone Racoon on the street and were intercepted by a Dog Patrol, one of the men was executed on the spot. If the Cats, or indeed the Lord High, thought that would curb the protests, it had the opposite effect, loosing more humans on the street.

The second man was killed for defying the Grey Guard, so the news sheets said. The third for what was vaguely defined as *anarchy*.

That last killing worried Livie the most. The other two Removals had involved what the mechanicals could consider direct actions. The last, what the man presumably thought or intended.

If they could be slaughtered for their thoughts, there

would soon be no humans left.

Things were tense in the houses where Livie cleaned. The House Mice watched her with intent black eyes and far less often left her to just get on with her work. It felt as if they waited for her to make a misstep.

The whole City waited, and their lives hung by a thread.

Benton told Livie it was the same at his job. No one met on the corners to talk any more. They were afraid to step into the taverns. Since he was perforce out on the street, he saw a lot of what happened. Mechanicals lorded it with increased confidence. Humans scurried.

She witnessed the next Removal, right out on the street, a spectacle she observed with horror. She had just finished her day's work and gone out to head for home. It was raining hard, the carriages that passed throwing up great gouts of water. A human standing in a group of others on the far side of the street from Livie took offense at being splashed and threw a rock—not at the carriage but at the mechanical Horse that pulled it. The Horse took umbrage in turn and halted of its own accord. Turned on the man.

He had no chance to run. No sooner did the Horse whinny out than a number of Dogs and Wolves converged on the man precisely as if they'd awaited such an occurrence.

The man, yelling and struggling, was dragged to the center of the street where the Horse denounced him. Passed sentence.

It was carried out by a member of the Grey Guard. Unlike the account in the broadsheet, this Wolf did not use his sword to stab the condemned through the heart.

He lopped off the man's head.

It was done swiftly and cleanly. The headless body dropped and the head rolled some distance, the eyes wide.

Women on the street screamed. Men cried out in protest.

But no one moved.

How might they? No saving the man, no saving anyone, and each of them might be next.

So much blood. Livie had never guessed there could be so much blood in a single human's veins.

Nor did she realize she had dropped to her knees till the wet soaked up through her skirt. She rose, staggering.

People began to move off silently. Livie followed suit. Her feet led her to her old room.

She found Gloria out of bed and making a cup of tea when she arrived. The woman still looked a fright with her stubble hair growing in patches and her gaunt, scarred face. But she moved under her own power.

"Olivia? Goodness, what is it?"

"Eh?"

"Ye're weepin'."

Was she? "I just saw—I just saw—"

Gloria made her sit down and gave her the tea. The broadsheets that Benton had brought and that Livie had passed on to Gloria lay spread around the room as if Gloria had been studying their contents.

Her dark eyes looked perfectly sane when they met Livie's. "What did ye see?"

"They killed a man. Removed him. Right there on the street."

Gloria's lips grew tight.

"I think it was because—"

"It doesn't matter why, does it?"

Livie shook her head. "There was so much blood."

"We do bleed. That's what sets us apart from them."

"I think I'm goin' to be sick."

"No." Gently, Gloria pushed Livie's head down to her knees. "Deep breaths."

A number of ragged breaths later, Gloria said musingly, "I used to vomit sometimes when they tortured me. I was afraid I'd choke on it. There were times I wished I would."

Livie raised her head. "Ye must be far stronger than me."

"I don't think so. Better now?"

"No. Yes. It's just that—one minute he was alive, shoutin' at them. The next—"

"They're bent on teachin' lessons. They like to do that. Since they're so good at learnin', at acceptin' instructions, they think we should be too. They forget about free will. That we can take notions in the head that don't answer to strict instruction."

"Yes."

"Sit a while."

"Nobody interfered. They—we all just stood there."

"Of course."

"I didn't dare—"

"No. Ye have somethin' to live for, don't ye? Your Benton."

Silently, Livie acknowledged that. Perhaps she did. "It seems we all have somethin' to live for," she said slowly, "no matter how deprived we may be. That poor man—"

"Yes, I'm sure he had much to live for. That too is part of our human condition. Drink your tea and listen to me."

But she didn't talk. She watched Livie drink the tea with a quiet intensity all out of proportion to the activity.

Only then did she say, "I've been thinkin'. Studyin' these broadsheets." She gestured at the papers. "Makin' some decisions. When is the next meetin' of the resistance?"

"I'm not sure."

"Find out for me. It's important that I be there."

"Is it?" Livie asked doubtfully.

"Yes. I still have my life, ye see—not like that man out on the street. It's important I use it for somethin'." Her eyes seemed to gaze inward. "No matter how dangerous."

When Livie, hurrying now, reached Benton's room sometime later, he was just leaving for work. They had time for only a few quick words there outside the building, in the rain.

He had heard about the Removal—word was all over the street—and could not believe she had witnessed it.

"Are ye all right?"

"Yes. I—stopped home. Gloria gave me some tea."

His lips quirked in what was not a true smile. "I wish I could stay with ye. Hold ye." He gave her a single hard kiss. "I dare not be late."

"No, don't be late." For one moment, she clutched at him. "Don't step wrong. Ye—ye are precious to me."

It was the closest she could come to admitting how she felt about him. As she watched him hurry off through the rain, she hoped he understood.

To say an air of panic pervaded the streets would not be an overstatement. It simmered like a fever, spreading from human to human through the rain, nearly tangible as Benton worked his rounds. Few of them spoke about it. Few dared to linger long enough. The presence of the Dog Police had increased, all of them patrolling in pairs, and no one wanted to draw their attention.

Yet whenever he encountered another man, Benton saw the fear in his eyes. An exchange of a look took place before they moved on.

Even the taverns seemed empty. Those on his route failed to give off their usual clamor, and their lights shone dim on the wet pavement.

People, when able, were gone home. Gone to ground, in the face of this new danger. And who could blame them? He longed to be at home with Olivia, in his own bed. Not doing anything beyond holding her, clinging to her the way she had to him for that moment before they parted.

Would she be all right alone after witnessing an execution? How long would it be before they all witnessed one?

It could not become commonplace. Could not be allowed to. But what could any human do?

He went straight home after finishing his shift and caught Olivia just preparing to rise. He shed his wet clothing and just for an instant crawled into the bed with her, the blankets warm and smelling of her. She absorbed his chill, which went right to his bones, before hurrying up to go to her job.

He lay there after she left, and tried unsuccessfully to sleep. The rain beat against his window, a sound that usually served to lull him but in this instance failed. Too many thoughts crammed his head. Too many fears. Where could their world go from here? How much worse could it get?

He slept little and rose early so he could walk out and meet Olivia at the end of her workday. He now knew her schedule, where she cleaned on which days, and was in time to take her bucket from her.

She brightened only slightly at the sight of him.

"Hard day?" he asked.

She nodded. Her shoulders slumped and she looked so downhearted, he wound an arm around her.

"Want to stop for a drink?"

"No. Let's just get home."

Once again, the taverns they passed were half empty and they saw few humans on the streets, though the numbers of mechanicals abounded, as if they expanded to fill the space left by the humans they barely deigned to notice.

People were toeing the line, staying in. When they reached Benton's room, Olivia moved into his arms.

"Do we have time to—?"

"Yes."

"I don't want to make ye late."

They made quick, desperate love in the bed, as if throwing their humanity into the face of a storm. As he came inside her, Benton thought about the folly of it. He did not want her to conceive his child. She did not want it either. Or, on some basic, instinctive level, did they? This was no time to bring a child into the world. This world.

And yet did he unconsciously, as a last act, seek to further the race? Leave a part of himself, should he be the next to be Removed?

"I needed that." Olivia gave him a long, lingering kiss at variance with their fast, brilliant mating. "I needed ye."

"Yes." He moved his hand against the softness of her breast, easing his abused palm. "Olivia, I hope ye know how I feel about ye—"

"I hope ye know also. It's a miracle we found each other amid all this."

Need they say more than that? Need he speak the word *love*?

As he went out to begin his rounds that night, he heard the whispers. The furtive exchanges of information. A new declaration on the part of the Lord High had been pinned up at various locations, and Donkeys went about the city decrying it for those who could not read.

Since Benton could, he stopped by the nearest post and perused it. A long scroll, it had been nailed up with a transparent sheet over it to protect it from the rain.

It listed the names of those who had, so far, been Removed—fully five of them now—and proclaimed:

*Protests will not be tolerated.*

*Rebellion will not be tolerated.*

*Harm to any mechanical will result in immediate Removal.*

*No exceptions.*

Immediate. Immediate removal. No time for pleas or explanations. No excuses. A man who might well have reason to speak for himself—*my mate needs me*—would be dead before the words could leave his lips.

He shivered as he stood there in the rain. Then he moved off rapidly, terrified to his boots that he would be late to his shift, and give them a reason.

Even though they did not truly need one.

## Chapter Fifteen

"What are ye?" Gloria demanded coldly, reasonably, and without anger. "Are ye men and women? Or are ye frightened children hidin' in the dark?"

Those to whom she spoke, once more gathered in the upstairs room of the tavern where Danny worked, gazed at her in silent misgiving. With a dazed kind of wonder. Not one responded.

It had been Gloria who'd called the meeting, or insisted that Olivia have it called. People were afraid now to gather. Terrified of discovery. Yet neither did they want to admit they lacked the courage to do so. The usuals had filtered in one by one, when word of the meeting spread. None of them appeared eager.

In the time it had taken to arrange the meeting, two more Removals had occurred, both very visible out on the street.

People were justifiably frightened, the taverns still half empty.

Now Gloria wobbled on her weak legs at the head of the room, only her dark eyes appearing strong. Fierce.

"Look at me," she invited, spreading her arms. "See what they did to me. If I can find the courage to defy them, why can't ye?"

They were looking, and none of them wanted to be her. Expressions of dismay, dread, and outright horror twisted their features.

Still no one spoke.

"Those whom the Lord High has set above us," Gloria went on in her soft yet sharp-edged voice, "know nothin' of mercy. That is because they do not fear as we do—or feel as we do. Indeed, they possess only knowledge that he has instilled in them, includin' the knowledge that they are above us. Better than us. Do ye not see? He has deliberately and for reasons of his own instituted a reversal of the age-old belief that man was at the top of the food chain. Granted by God the right to lord it over animals as he chose. To hurt them and farm them and slay them out of hand, for food or to make the shoes on his feet, the clothin' on his back, or whatever purpose we saw fit.

"I am not sayin'," she added a bit more intently, "I fail to see or recognize the Lord High's purpose. It is his methods with which I take exception. For in days gone by, not all of us were merciless. There were those who listened to their hearts. Who lifted up the fallen creatures and sought to help them. Who intervened in the cruelty and did their best to stop it.

"Now we all, all of us humans, suffer the same treatment. But our weakness may also be our strength."

"How's that, miss?" asked a man from the back of the room.

Gloria fastened her gaze on him. "Because we feel, we may be able to outsmart them. And because the Lord High is also a human, he may have made a fatal mistake."

"A mistake? Him?" Danny raised an eyebrow. "Of what sort?"

Gloria drew a breath, wobbled a little on her weak legs and sank to a bench behind her. Those who listened followed her with their eyes.

"Not many of ye know I used to work for him, for the Lord High. In the palace, I did, as a young girl, because I came from a prosperous family and could read and write very well. I was as my name implies, a Clark. And I learned much of the Lord High who is, so I do promise ye, truly a man."

No one made a sound. That last statement, they did not necessarily believe.

Her lips twisted. "A man who has achieved ultimate power. I copied the texts that detailed his thoughts, his messages to others. The records of his work.

"He wanted to preserve the animals, yes, after the Great Killing nearly destroyed the world. He did not care so much for us. Being human, he built into those mechanical animals the very characteristics their long-gone flesh-and-blood counterparts had once possessed. The mechanical Wolves resemble and replicate the wolves of old—fast, strong, silent, and deadly. Just as his Foxes are canny and his Dogs live to serve. None of them *feel*—not as we do—but they follow an ancient blueprint of feeling.

"This mistake on the part of the Lord High may save us."

"How?" It was Benton, standing beside Olivia, who spoke. He'd best leave soon or he'd be late to start his shift. And Olivia did not want that.

Risky enough being here at all. What if a pair of dutiful Dobermans found them, or a patrolling Wolf?

Gloria fastened her gaze to Benton. "These small characteristics the Lord High could not resist building into his creations are their weaknesses. We know—or can guess—how they will react. We may use that against them."

Her listeners shifted for the first time and glanced at one another.

Olivia felt daunted. Unsure, even though Gloria seemed so certain about what she said. Was she merely mad, after all?

"Think about it," Gloria went on, urging them. "Has any of ye ever known a Cat, for instance, to act in any way but superior? To do anythin' but despise us? No. They do not stray from their expected behaviors. They cannot. It is written into their very mechanics and will not change. We can use that predictability."

"How?" Benton asked again.

"Look at me," Gloria invited once again, leading Olivia to, yes, wonder about her sanity. "Do ye think they did this to me for no reason? Do ye suppose they did their best to destroy not only my body but my mind out of fancy? No, it was because I had stumbled on secret knowledge—there while glimpsin' the Lord High's notes, I did. And if ye swear to me—one and all—that ye will fight for our liberty, I will share it with ye all."

\*\*\*\*

"Do ye think she is mad?" Olivia expressed the thought that possessed her to Benton a short while later as she walked him to the start of his route. Dark had nearly fallen, and the rain fell hard. They had to huddle close for him to hear her. "Do ye think that's what we saw back there—the cracks in her mind?"

"Don't know," Benton admitted. "She seemed very sure of what she said."

"And yet—they did destroy her mind back in those torture chambers, right? They would never have released her if they weren't sure she'd forgotten any secrets she might have glimpsed among the Lord High's notes."

"Or," Benton stopped walking. They had reached his first lamp post. "She merely let them think so."

"How could anyone endure such pain and not break? How not confess anythin' to make it stop?"

"I don't know." It would take enormous strength, far more than Benton suspected he himself possessed. "If she does have knowledge and we could exploit it—"

Olivia backed off a step. "It's dangerous."

"What we've been doin', resistin', was always dangerous."

"Doubly so now that we can be killed out of hand."

"Yes."

"Kiss me. I need a kiss from ye before our night apart."

A demand with which Benton was glad to comply. Her lips felt warm in the wet, chilly night. She tasted sublime.

"Ye'd best get home, love. Go safely."

But she clutched his forearms. "Say that again."

"What?"

"What ye called me. Love."

"Love."

"I love ye, Benton."

He melted from the toes upward. Standing in the downpour he felt the warmth flow through him. "And I love ye."

They kissed once, twice, thrice. Something upon which to live.

"Go safely," he repeated.

"Work safely."

He watched her disappear through the hard rain before climbing up the first pole, coaxing the light. He brought light to the dark. Could he also be a part of what brought liberation to mankind?

He wanted that, he did. But he wanted Olivia's safety more, feared endangering her far more than himself. Whether or not he believed what Gloria had told them, he feared he lacked the woman's strength.

She spoke of weaknesses, and yes, that was one on his part. He feared for the woman he loved.

He'd never dreamed, so he thought as his palms rasped the rough surface of the metal pole, that anyone would love him, truly love him as Olivia did. That she would desire him, offer him her body and her heart.

He could not bear to lose that.

Yet—yet if the Lord High and his mechanicals had anything to do about it, he could lose her anyway. One or the other of them might be summarily executed. So even if he might be content to live and survive only on Sundays, there were no guarantees they would be allowed so much as that.

The rules could change at any moment. They might be denied even Sundays.

He would gladly work for her till he dropped. Die for her. Would he risk what they had, for the ultimate good?

A harder prospect.

Did he believe Gloria? Or was she mad and raving? She had chosen to drop her great secret onto a ragged-ass group of—in Benton's eyes—piss-poor members of an obscure branch of the resistance. She might do better. They might *be* better.

If it were true—

The thing was, the thing that convinced him was that Olivia herself had touched upon the same truth, in an earlier meeting. Before she'd gone to prison and met

Gloria Clarkwoman.

Coincidence? Maybe. Maybe not.

He needed to consider on it. Without the tangle of emotions getting in the way. Yet his emotions were severely tangled and he did not suppose he could completely disregard them.

Love, fear, protectiveness, desire. They accompanied him up and down every pole as he worked through his night, and left him aching.

The streets remained fairly quiet that night, the taverns he passed mostly empty, people frightened enough to stay home. Increased Dog patrols were in evidence and each time they swiveled a mechanical eye to him, Benton flinched. The Grey Guard would be around—unseen.

Mechanicals too had curtailed their former celebrations. Some carriages carrying Cats rumbled past and a few groups of Foxes emerged from the clubs. But Benton's main companion was the rain.

He went straight home after his shift, hoping to catch Olivia. Praying they might have time for a quick exchange in the warm bed—for he was chilled right through—or at least another kiss.

But his stark little room lay empty, only her scent lingering there. She must have gone out to work early, afraid of reprisals.

It was no way to live, especially for the woman he loved.

****

"Do ye think they believed me?" Gloria asked Olivia, who stood just inside the door of her former room. "Or do they suppose me just a madwoman?"

Olivia did not know what to say. She'd left Benton's

room early so she could stop by and make sure Gloria was all right. That had been a strenuous session back above the tavern. And perhaps she wanted to reassure herself about a few other things.

"I'm not sure," she replied. "Ye did not choose the brightest bunch, if I'm honest, upon whom to drop your—er—secret. They're a simple lot, really. Joinin' in the resistance for the sake of it, more than anythin'."

Gloria shot her a look. She seemed different, somehow, from the broken woman who had languished in the narrow bed. Lit from within. Purposeful. "They're what we have to work with. They'll have to get hold of themselves and step up."

"We."

Olivia did not realize she'd spoken the word till Gloria faced her.

"Don't ye believe me either? Do ye still think me damaged in my mind?"

"Not damaged, no." Not entirely. "But—are ye sure about what ye remember? Ye said your memories were ruined. By the torture."

Not without passion, Gloria said, "I had to claim that, didn't I? Don't ye see? I never would have got out if I hadn't convinced them I forgot what I knew."

"But ye didn't forget."

"I managed to hang on to some vital knowledge, yes. Even while they tried to burn it from me. Do ye understand what that cost?"

Olivia let her gaze rove over the scars. "I think so. At least, I can imagine."

"I knew how important it was. This is my chance. *Ye* are my chance."

Olivia went dizzy. "But I'm just an ordinary—"

"If ye say ordinary woman, I will hit ye. So was I. We can none of us afford to be what ye might call ordinary."

They stared at one another.

"I'm sorry," Olivia whispered then. "Sorry for what ye've suffered and for…"

"For doubtin' me?" Gloria did not blink.

"For wonderin', only, if what ye suffered did turn your mind."

"Ye think I would make up what I told ye and the others?"

Olivia shrugged. "It's a well-guarded secret."

"Excellently guarded," Gloria agreed, "which is why they did what they did to me."

"I still don't understand why they did not just kill ye."

"Neither do I. As I say, there were times I begged for it. And maybe that is why. My torturers wanted to see, and learn, how far they could push me and when my mind would break."

"And ye convinced them it had."

"Yes. Olivia—" She reached out. "Believe I would never lie to ye."

"I do believe that. Ye would not lie to me intentionally, but under duress there is a possibility the mind could invent, well, anythin'."

"Then your group, your resistance—"

"Our resistance."

"Will have to prove it to ye. A capture. Follow-through."

Olivia thought about that. It caused a shudder. "And if it isn't true? If it doesn't work?"

"It will."

"Those makin' the venture will be killed immediately, out of hand."

"Ye think they—your group—have not the courage for it?"

"I'm not sure."

"Perhaps Benton—"

"Not him."

"He seems capable. Courageous."

"Not him." Anyone but him.

Gloria drew herself up. "Ye don't believe me."

"Ye're askin' me to risk Benton's life."

"It's already at risk. Every time he's out there." She gestured at the door.

Tears flooded Olivia's eyes. "I need him."

"More than your freedom?"

A good question, one to which Olivia did not know if she had the answer.

****

Come Sunday morning, Olivia waited impatiently for Benton to return from his shift, pacing the tight confines of the little room and listening to the rain hit the window. Since the meeting above the tavern, they'd been like moons passing in the heavens, and she wanted a chance to talk to him properly. Discuss what Gloria had told her and what she asked.

Their world had become a place where one feared to step wrong, to violate a rule by being late, by a word or a look. No one took the chance of lingering for an extra reassurance or kiss. A terrible sort of order had come into place, one not of their making.

But Olivia's nerves had frayed as her fear chewed at her the way rodents once had, for now they stood shoulder-high and dealt in secondhand garbage.

When the lock on the door rattled, she nearly jumped out of her skin. Benton came in shedding water.

He looked weary, and that said a lot. Ever since Olivia had met him, back when she'd joined the group, he'd seemed solid as a mountain, nearly unflappable, with a steady energy. Now his wide shoulders slumped beneath the weight of his kit bag. He seemed to move more slowly than usual, and even his lips drooped with discontent.

Olivia flew to his arms. She had meant to give him a moment or two to regain himself, to shrug off the labors of his night and the uncertainty of the streets. Yet so glad was she to see him come in, to have him with her, she moved by instinct and burrowed in tight.

"Here, now," he cried. "Ye'll get yourself all wet."

She would, she did. The rain clinging to his coat soaked into her and it felt cold. She didn't care and burrowed in harder till he wrapped his arms around her and gave a breathless half laugh.

"All right."

With her ear snug against his chest, she could hear his heart beating, steady and oh, so human. She'd been longing to talk to him. She needed to talk to him, wanted the sense and reassurance of it. Once in his arms, though, she discovered she needed something else more.

She lifted her lips to his, and he dove for them. With helpless devotion, they claimed each other once again, seeking the comfort of it. For Olivia, the rest of the world and its accompanying worries took a step backward.

"Well," Benton moaned against her lips, "this is a greetin' I like."

"Do ye?"

"Oh, yes."

"Come to the bed with me."

"I'm soaking wet."

She stripped the clothing from him, hanging each dripping garment on a peg on the wall, for even under the spear of desire clothing remained valuable. His hair still sopping, she towed him to the bed.

"Olivia, I'll get the sheets all—"

"Let me dry ye."

She did so, using her tongue and her lips, sucking the wet from every part of him till he complained no more. Between forays across his skin she shed articles of her own clothing and when he climaxed, this time in her mouth, she too found her satisfaction.

The air in the room grew chilly then, with both of them damp. They cuddled close and Benton drew the shabby blanket over them.

"What was that about?" he mused in a deep rumble.

"I missed ye."

"So I could tell." At variance with when he'd entered the room only moments before, a smile colored his voice. "I missed ye also."

"Benton. Benton." She drew herself up from his chest so she could peer into his face. That broad face, so ordinary. So extraordinary. Those eyes she'd once deemed plain as mud now speckled with amber.

"I love ye so. More than I ever thought I could."

She felt the breath catch in his chest. Brighter light flared in his eyes, and he stroked her hair tenderly.

"And I love ye."

"Maybe—maybe," she declared, fighting against the darkness, "that's all that matters. That we love and are loved. That we find someone in this world to trust."

"Perhaps it is."

But behind the great love brimming in his eyes, she beheld the doubt. And despite all she felt for him, an echo of it reverberated in her own heart.

## Chapter Sixteen

Benton lay with his heart pounding in his ears and the memory of pleasure tingling across his skin. He could still feel Olivia's mouth upon him everywhere it had been. Gathering moisture across his chest, plowing through the hair there. Caressing each shoulder. Easing the pain that persisted in the palms of his hands. When she moved lower, ever lower to enfold him in the warmth of her mouth, he'd given himself over to the ecstasy of it and released himself there.

Now they cuddled tight, as close as two could be, and the comfort of it near stunned him, yet the memory of the night past hovered in his mind.

No matter. They had a whole day together, and if he loved her enough, the memory should fade.

She lifted her head from his shoulder and looked into his eyes, her own wide and silvery blue. So beautiful, was his woman with her hair tumbled around her shoulders and the traces of him still on her tongue.

"I love ye," she said. A pronouncement. A reassurance and a vow.

As it did every time she made the confession, the breath caught in his chest and his heartbeat accelerated impossibly.

"And I love ye," he assured her instantly, because it was true. He'd never imagined loving anyone or anything as he did her.

"Maybe, as I said, that's all that matters," she proposed tentatively, "that we love and are loved. That we find someone in this world to trust."

"Perhaps it is." But there was more, for a man who loved. There was the desire to protect, and that had been taken from him. The very right to defend his own had been stolen. She might not understand that, but he felt it to the bone.

Could she sense that all his heart was not in the words he spoke? Possibly, for she pressed her mouth to his. He could taste himself on her tongue.

"Love," he told her when the long, luxurious kiss ended, "is a wondrous thing. A prize, indeed, to find in this world. And I do prize ye—"

"Let's get married. Make it official, a pledge and a promise."

"Olivia, darlin', I could not be more promised to ye if I tried."

That made her smile. "Yes, I know. I believe that. I trust in it. But swearin' it official would be a—a kind of bulwark against the world."

"If that is what ye want," he ran his fingers through her hair, "that is what we shall do."

"Like spittin' in the eye of fate, isn't it?"

"Yes." He had fallen into the depths of what he saw in her eyes and did not suppose he could get out again. Even if he wanted to.

"When? How?"

Benton didn't know. Marriages between humans were tolerated by the mechanicals but not always recognized. He did not know that it would actually serve to protect them.

He could do nothing, so it seemed, to defend their

love.

"I will inquire. See if I can discover who is still performing the ceremonies."

"You. Do. That." Each word came punctuated with a soft kiss. She lay sprawled atop him, her naked breasts pressed to his skin. Desire rose in a staggering wave.

"Meanwhile, make love to me."

He did, giving the whole of his heart over to it, worshipping her as she had him, in turn. He wished he could live like this always, moment by moment, feeling the swollen flesh of her nipples grow taut against his tongue, absorbing her need and losing himself in her heat when he plunged into her.

Man for woman, woman for man. Perfection. If only there were nothing more.

"We must be wed soon, *soon*," she told him after he came inside her. "There may be a child."

That made him blink and peer into her eyes. "Are ye—"

"Too soon to tell. But given what has been happenin', what just happened…"

"Yes." Him, a father, with another precious life he would not be able to protect.

"There is somethin' else I must discuss with ye," Olivia whispered, her passions if not her fears temporarily soothed. "We have not truly had a chance to talk about what Gloria said at the meetin'."

"Yes." Dismay roiled in his gut. "I confess, I've been thrustin' it to the back of my mind."

"But we can't, can we?"

"I suppose not."

"Benton, do ye believe her?"

A good question. He'd seen the expressions on the

faces of her listeners the other night, and felt the emotions in the room. He didn't know that anyone believed her.

Or disbelieved.

"She was convincin'," he said slowly. "But she has been through a lot. And the mechanicals deemed her mad enough, and thus safe enough to release."

"Yes, but they're mechanicals, aren't they? Her whole point is that they can be fooled."

"Maybe. Maybe they can." It had not been Benton's experience.

"Do ye think it's true?" Olivia pressed.

"I don't know. Do ye?"

"When I admitted to my doubts, she grew very indignant. Said she'd hung on to the knowledge at great cost."

Benton stirred uneasily in the bed. "Is that even possible? In the old days, people would confess to crimes they had not committed under torture. Things like heresy. And witchcraft."

"Treason."

"I imagine so. How are we to suppose she, a frail woman, could endure?"

"But, Benton, if she did? It would change everythin', give us a way to fight back. Not—not just talk about resistance but do somethin' to resist. Because if we could begin to eliminate them—"

"Can we?" Now Benton focused on that completely, chilled despite the warmth of her in his arms. "Wouldn't the Lord High just repair any we're able to turn off? He built them, after all."

"It would take time, as it did in the beginnin'. Remember, there are tales of the Great Killing and how the world was near deserted after, until he built his creatures to repopulate it. People lived like animals and—"

"The animals he created lived high, like people." Benton finished for her. "He's been playin' at bein' God."

"And now, if Gloria is right, we have one of God's secrets."

"If she is right."

"I guess what it comes down to," said Olivia, playing with his fingers that lay over her naked stomach, "is how brave are we? All this while, in our meetin's and in our hearts, we've been talkin' about findin' ways to fight back. Now that we have that chance—will we?"

****

It seemed to be a question shared by all those who had heard Gloria speak in the room above the tavern. Olivia bumped into one of them on the street the next day when she was going from one assignment to the next. She dodged a puddle, nearly collided with someone, and regarded him.

A man called Freddie he was, one who had attended every meeting and sometimes spoke verbosely about the need to resist. Now, as he recognized Olivia, he started and gave a furtive glance around.

"Livie? How is your friend? The one who—"

"She's doin' all right. Still recoverin'."

The Dog Police, who patrolled endlessly, would allow them to exchange a few words before becoming suspicious, but just doing so made Olivia grow tense. Imagine a world, she thought, where humans didn't have to worry about doing as they pleased.

"I admit," Freddie went on, "I haven't been able to

get what she told us out of my mind." He lowered his voice so she could barely hear him above the rain. "Do ye think it's true?"

Olivia shook her head, but not in denial. "I've been wonderin' also."

"She seemed very certain, and yet—"

And yet.

Freddie hurried on, "If it is true, well, we've been waitin' for just such information, haven't we? We can't waste it."

That was one of the conclusions to which Olivia had also come, after her conversation with Benton. "No. morally, we can't waste it."

"Otherwise," Freddie said seriously, "we've been lyin' to ourselves all this time."

"Just so." From the corner of her eye, Olivia saw a Police Dog turn its attention to them.

"Listen, Fred, I have to go. Can't be late to my next post, right?"

He blinked at her. "Fred. No one's called me that in a man's age."

She smiled and hurried off.

Her next assignment belonged to the Ferrets, and dread stirred in her gut when she let herself in. She still felt uneasy when she thought of them, though she'd encountered them but seldom since her time in prison.

Now she sighed silently as she saw the condition of the foyer floor, the very place of her downfall. Mud splashes and shoe prints trailed it from side to side as if the occupants had been walking along the river since she'd last turned this floor spotless. All at once a wave of weary discouragement overtook her. What was the point of swabbing if her employers made no effort to keep the area clean?

No point, save that she was a Scrubwoman and, in the eyes of her employers, worth nothing more than a set of hands to clean their filth.

She removed her coat and hung it, dripping, beside the door, tiptoed off to fill her bucket in the kitchen where the House Mice eyed her as if she'd crawled out of the woodwork.

When she returned to the foyer, Melia Ferret stood in the doorway of the parlor, drawn up as tall as a Ferret could be.

"There you are," Melia declared. "You're late."

She wasn't, despite the stolen moments with Freddie, but she did not say so. She wanted no more trouble with this mechanical.

"Get to work. This floor is filthy, and we've special guests tonight."

"Yes, Madam Ferret."

"I want it spotless, mind."

"Yes."

The Ferret went away back into the parlor and Olivia sighed again. She heard music coming from the parlor—for some reason mechanicals enjoyed music—and the tune accompanied her as she worked, crawling inch by inch across the filthy floor, sponging away the thick traces of mud, careful to avoid the little table that had caused her downfall before.

She was nearly done, the marble tiles gleaming behind her when Melia reappeared from the parlor. The Ferret stood for a moment, her small, dark eyes examining Olivia's efforts, before she spoke.

"Unacceptable."

"What?" From her position on her hands and knees,

Olivia craned her head to look around. "But—" Every trace of mud was gone.

"You vengeful wretch," Melia accused. "You refuse to do your best work for me because we sent you to prison."

"No." This was Olivia's best work.

"The floor is not shiny. There is a fog."

"No." Even from where she knelt, Olivia could see the tiles gleaming.

"What did you say to me?" Melia sallied forth from the doorway and across the still damp floor, up to where Olivia knelt.

"Ma'am, the floor is quite shiny."

"It is not." With one well-aimed kick, Melia booted Olivia's bucket onto its side. Filthy water splashed everywhere, including on Olivia, and began making a trail across the floor. The water in the bucket, more mud than anything else, turned the tiles brown in an ill tide.

"There." Melia screeched. "Now is it clean?"

*Do not lose your temper*, Olivia warned herself. *Do not retaliate*. She began to climb to her feet but never had the chance. Melia's second kick took her in the side and knocked her over onto the wet floor. The mechanical had small paws clad in fashionable shoes, but the fur had steel inside it, and the force created by steam mechanics.

Melia's next kick took Olivia in the shoulder hard enough to earn a grunt. In an effort to try and protect herself, Olivia flipped onto her knees and forearms. The fourth and fifth kicks took her in the belly, driving sharply upward into the soft tissue there.

Pain stunned her and she collapsed onto the flooded floor, trying to protect her belly.

Melia screeched at her, "Now clean this up, you

worthless sack of excrement. And do a proper job this time."

She left. It took Olivia several minutes to ascertain that yes, the Ferret had gone and to haul herself up. A pair of House Mice, drawn from the kitchen by the racket, stood at the back of the foyer, goggling at her. Neither offered so much as a paw to help as Olivia dragged herself up, hurting.

She wanted to wail in protest. She wanted to flee. She stood with her hands clutched to her belly and eyed the flooded floor, her work wholly destroyed.

She had to return to the kitchen for clean water. The House Mice, withdrawn there, ignored her as if she did not exist.

She wept into her hands as she scrubbed, and even before she finished redoing the floor she could feel that she bled. Not from the site of the blows, where bruises no doubt spread, but between her legs.

With the floor shining, she fled out at last and into the rain.

Chapter Seventeen

She went to her old room because it was closer than Benton's. Gloria took one look at her and drew her in, alarm flooding her dark eyes.

"Olivia? My dear, what is it? What has happened?"

Olivia told her in broken words while Gloria removed her sopping coat and coaxed her to sit down, ending with, "I'm bleedin'. I think she hurt me inside."

The next moments proved chaotic. The chamber pot was employed and an old sheet sacrificed to mop the blood, which came profusely.

Gloria tended Olivia with quick, efficient hands. When the worst of the agony stemmed, she asked, "Olivia, was it your time of the month?"

Olivia shook her head.

"Is there any chance ye were pregnant?"

*Were.* Had she bled out Benton's child?

"Ye think I've—I've miscarried?"

Gloria's face grew tight. "No way to tell. Ye wouldn't have been very far along, would ye?"

"No. Benton and I—Benton and I just started livin' together—" But yes, they'd rashly stopped being careful about that. Had even mentioned the possibility of a child.

"That was an awful lot of blood," Gloria said with careful sympathy. "No way now to tell."

No way to tell, either way. Cruelty, though…sheer cruelty might have cost her something dear.

She dissolved into tears. Gloria let her weep until the wild storm eased. Then Gloria said, "Where is Benton now? Do ye want me to go find him?"

"No." What time was it? How much time had passed in this horror? "He'll be headin' to work soon. I—there's no point in troublin' him."

"I think I should try and fetch a physician. Just in case, in case—" Gloria repeated, "That was a terrible lot of blood."

Human doctors were few, and though some would attend out of pity, others were hideously expensive.

"No. The worst of it has passed now. But she hurt me, Gloria. She hurt me bad." A dull kind of anger rose up out of the grief.

"I know she did."

"I hate her. *Hate* her." Olivia rolled over in the bed and her gaze found that of Gloria, who hovered above. "I want her shut off. Shut down. I want them all shut down." She was willing now to believe Gloria's claims. Rage brought a kind of strength that allowed for it.

"Yes," Gloria told her. "They will be. One at a time."

\*\*\*\*

When Benton arrived home from work the next morning to find Gloria outside his building with her shorn head showing and her wasted body wrapped in a coat made from a blanket, he shied in surprise. Dismay came striding on its heels. Gloria would not be here unless something terrible had happened.

"What is it?" he asked with alarm. "Where's Olivia?"

"I think ye had better come with me."

They went slowly, much more slowly than Benton

would have liked due to Gloria's debility. On the way she told him what had happened. And his anger welled, all mixed with the familiar frustration.

"D'ye know if it was—if there was a child?"

"Too early. Impossible to tell."

"Have ye secured a doctor?"

"She won't let me."

"I'll pay for one," Benton said rashly.

"She insists the worst is over, and it is. The bleedin' has near stopped. She also insists she's all right. She isn't. She's—shattered."

"Yes," Benton said helplessly.

"May I ask ye a question?" Gloria slanted a look at him.

"Go ahead."

"What were ye thinkin', takin' a chance on impregnatin' her, with the way things are?"

It was asked matter-of-factly rather than offensively, and Benton did not take umbrage. He shook his head. "I do not suppose I was thinkin'."

"Well, ye'd best start."

"We are plannin' to marry. As soon as possible."

"I see."

"As for—for the child—" For an instant, Benton lost his train of thought. If there had been a child, what would that child have been like? Would it have had Olivia's blue-gray eyes? Her smile? His height?

Lost, now, if ever it had existed. Lost. "I could kill that Ferret," he growled.

"Better to put your energy into shuttin' them down. It's what she wants, Olivia."

"Is it?"

"Yes. She wants it so bad, she's decided she believes

me." Another look slanted up at him. "Do ye?"

"Let me put it this way. I also want to."

"Then use this, Benton. Use it to fuel your urge to fight."

At the door of the building, Benton eyed her. If this woman, scarred and tormented, could find the will and courage still to battle, why not he?

Up in Olivia's former room, now littered with broadsheets, he did his best to talk Olivia into letting him fetch a doctor, to no avail.

"It's over now," she told him, and wept. "If we had a child, it's gone."

Anger and helpless rage tore through him again. Seeing her this way—grief brimming in her eyes and her face streaked with tears—yes, he could fight. If not for this, then why?

"I just want to go home."

He carried her there in his arms with his pack slapping his back. Took her up to the tiny room where the rain clattered against the window, and tucked her into the bed.

She held out her arms to him. "Please. Hold me."

So he did, and all the while she wept, saying she had to get up and go to work.

"Ye cannot," he told her, kissing her heated cheeks and brow.

"I must. What if I'm late and they send me back to prison?"

"Send a message. Say ye're ill." They were allowed two days a year.

He was unable to talk her into a physician, but he did persuade her to send that message even though she protested, "They'll dock my wages for it."

"Let them."

"I'm already so far in debt."

As were they all, man and woman.

She bled so heavily, he had to help her change the bandaging several times. Other than that, they stayed in the bed and he dozed while she took refuge in his arms.

Late in the afternoon, he went out for food and they sat in the bed to eat.

"I'm so angry at Melia Ferret," Olivia said then, "I don't know how I'll face her again."

That made Benton's own anger surge. "I wish ye didn't have to, that ye could walk away from there. Ye could lodge a complaint."

"And make her hate me even more? Besides, the Cats who hear those complaints always side with the mechanicals. Nothin' ever gets changed."

It was true.

"What do ye think he or she would have been like, our daughter or son?"

Benton did not want to admit this had been on his mind, and further her grief. "Now, we don't know there was a child at all."

"Still and all."

"It would have been beautiful, like ye."

That made her turn and look at him with puffy eyes. "Ye said that before. D'ye still think me beautiful?"

"Oh, yes. I think ye be the most beautiful woman in the world."

It won him a shaky smile.

"Olivia, darlin', there will be other babes if ye want them." He could give her that. "I know it won't make up for— Well. And the way ye were treated." The brutality of it fair sickened him.

"I want revenge, Benton." She whispered it.

"I do too."

"Do ye think Gloria can give it to us?"

"We'll see."

**** 

The next time the group met, on another Saturday night over the tavern, the mood had changed. People were far more serious, and less uncertain. Nobody made bad jokes. Even the noise from the tavern, still half empty, was muted.

Olivia had been back to work by then. She dared not miss more than one day. Her body protested the long day's work, her mind wanted to fold in upon itself. But her spirit—her spirit took strength from anger.

She saw the same light in the others' eyes, especially after Gloria, who was also there, requested that Olivia should tell what had happened to her. The members had brought others, word of what Gloria had previously shared with them spreading. Never had the small room been packed so tight.

It was Danny, rather surprisingly, who discussed ways and means. Usually a charmer and a philanderer, he had gone dead serious, a sharp look in his eyes.

"I propose we capture one of them, as an experiment like, and see if it's true, what Madam Gloria says." He spoke the *Madam* as a sign of respect. "Not that I doubt ye, Madam Gloria, but before we set wider plans into motion, I feel it would be wise to make sure."

Gloria nodded. "Ye want to prove it to yourselves. I understand that."

"But it's dangerous," one of the men ventured. "Snatchin' one of our betters off the street."

"They're not our betters," Freddie growled.

"Ye know what I mean."

They all did.

Benton said, "They have no hesitation in treatin' us any way they choose. I say we return the favor."

Several of his fellow Lightmen, who had joined the meeting, nodded their agreement.

"So," Danny reasoned, "we snatch one. A Cat. Because those are the plans Madam Gloria saw."

"Yes," Gloria said. "Though I'm sure the details are likely the same for all the models. Why would the Lord High alter a schematic that works, just because it's a different animal?"

"We don't know for sure," Marty Coffin said.

They knew nothing for sure and wouldn't till they had a mechanical in their hands.

"Ye doubt me." Gloria said it without resentment. "Ye look at me and ye think, she could be mad. So yes, snatch a Cat and prove it to yourselves."

"The trick," Olivia heard herself say, "will be catchin' one on its own. They're usually in groups, or at least in pairs."

"Some of the Toms go out alone at night," said Andy Lightman. "We see them on our rounds."

"Yes, but a Tom wouldn't be easy to capture. They can put up an awful fight."

"As can any of them," Freddie agreed. "There's steel beneath that soft fur, and the Lord High made sure to give them claws which are also steel. Can rake a man's eyes out."

An uncomfortable silence fell.

"Who's brave enough?" Danny asked them.

"Olivia's right, it will be hard catchin' one on its own."

"We Lightmen are in the best position to spot one. And," Andy hesitated, glancing at Benton, "maybe capture one?"

*No*, Olivia thought immediately. *Not Benton.* If something went wrong…

To her horror, he nodded. "I'm willin'."

"Benton." It came from her in a whisper and he glanced at her.

"I'm willin'," he repeated.

"All right. Two of us, or three. Now let's plan where to take 'im once we have 'im."

They discussed it up one side and down the other. The meeting ran late, till the Lightmen had to leave for their rounds.

Out in the dark, Benton kissed Olivia. She clung to him.

"Ye will be careful?"

"As ever. Nothin' will happen tonight. As we discussed, we'll just keep our eyes peeled, look for a target."

"Yes. Benton, I'm afraid."

"So am I," he admitted. "But we can't continue doin' nothin'. We can't go on as we have."

"Do ye think we can trust everyone who was in the meetin'? If somebody talks…"

"Then we're all in trouble. But we have to try. We have to believe in Gloria and in each other."

Olivia nodded miserably. "I wish ye could come home with me."

"So do I."

Instead, Gloria walked Olivia home. The woman had grown stronger, and though she walked with the help of a cane, she said moving helped her gain agility.

Laura Strickland

"Do ye still doubt me?" she asked Olivia as they went slowly through the rain. Up ahead, through the gathering dark, Olivia could see Lightmen at their work. Just like Benton.

"No, I don't doubt ye. But tell me again how ye gained the information."

"It was after hours, when I was done with my copyin'. As I said, I got curious, stepped into the Lord High's private workshop, and looked where I shouldn't. Curiosity is a powerful force and a characteristic humans and Cats share. That's why I think this will work."

But why did it have to be Benton?

"What if he gets caught?"

"Benton?" Not one to mince words, Gloria said, "Then it will be the mines for him without a doubt. They won't waste a man his size in prison."

"The mines. Till he dies."

"Yes." Gloria sighed.

"I don't think I could bear it."

"Ye'd be surprised what ye can bear."

****

The rain slackened off that night, which made it easy for Benton to search out targets. He kept his eyes peeled while he climbed up and down the poles, up and down, operating by rote.

He saw plenty of Cats. Unlike the humans, they were out in large numbers. But Olivia was right. They rarely traveled alone and often rode in carriages to spare their finery from the wet. Cats and water, as of old, did not mix.

They all appeared so civilized, it was hard to believe that one would fight if attacked. But he knew it to be true. The tentative plan, to swaddle the target in a cloak or

188

blanket, would definitely be called for.

Near the end of the night it was, that Benton spied him. A Tom, but not one out on the prowl. On foot, he instead appeared to be connected with the Council, one of the Court Justices perhaps, for he had that air, and he carried what might be a folded robe under his arm.

A member of the High Council? It would be folly to fall on such a one.

Yet he must be bound early for his chamber. If he went so every day—

Benton agonized over it. That would make him a likely candidate, if a risky one.

Not till the end of the night when he met up with Andy on his adjacent route, was he certain.

"Did ye see that hoity-toity Cat pass by?" Andy asked. "Headin' for the Council or the Palace, all on his own."

"I did."

Their eyes met and anger warred with stark terror in Benton's heart.

"Let's tell the others," Andy said.

Chapter Eighteen

They waited four nights and tracked the Tom's progress to make sure he was always out at that same early hour, and always alone. A creature of habit, so it seemed.

Messages flew far and wide among the members of the group. A location was chosen to take the captive—a cellar, near the river, where home brew was stored. Three men would waylay the Cat—Benton, Andy, and Danny who would loiter nearby. The other Lightmen would double up and cover the remainders of Benton's and Andy's routes.

Benton wavered over whether or not to tell Olivia they'd chosen a target. She still had not regained all her strength and struggled to get through her work days. He didn't want her worrying for him. In the end, he decided he preferred she hear the plan from him than from someone else in the group.

She wept when he told her, and glowed with both fear and anger. "Oh! Why does it have to be ye?"

"Why not me?"

He knew why not. Her heart bade her protect him even as he wanted to protect her. But they took this course precisely because they had no other way to protect each other.

"Wait with Gloria," he bade her. "If it works, if the kill switch is located where she says, we intend to switch him off and back on again. Then we'll return him to the street. If it goes well, he won't see us, bein' wrapped in the blanket."

"But he'll know he's been turned off and on, won't he? He'll tell. The Lord High will know that we have his secret."

"Yes."

"It will change everythin'. Put ye at risk. Put all of us at risk."

"Yes."

She said nothing. He could see the thoughts move in her eyes.

"Olivia, if we don't take this chance, where will we be? Helpless victims, as the Lord High makes more and more rules that allow his creatures to keep us down."

"I know that. My head does, but my heart—" She clutched at him. "I love ye so much."

Her love was a gift, a precious one. That much Benton knew. In their world, love and fear were sides of the same coin. He did not want her to live that way.

"I love ye also. Always." He wanted her to remember that. If something went wrong and he did not come back— "Wait with Gloria," he told her again. "Someone will bring word, all right?"

She agreed and walked with him to the start of his route before heading toward her old room. The night was cold and dark, mud splashing under foot and bootsteps echoing. It would be a long shift before the Cat appeared. If he appeared.

Too many thoughts crowded Benton's head as he worked through the night, up poles and down, shivering with chill and misgiving. He thought of the others with whom he'd be making this gamble. He thought of Olivia waiting this endless night through and of all the things that could go wrong.

What if Gloria was mistaken, or simply mad after all? If they seized the Cat off the street but could not find the switch to shut it down? Was that truly the highly guarded secret Gloria claimed to have glimpsed in the Lord High's records?

The Cat might see them. It would not forget. They would be doomed.

By the time he completed his rounds and started over, extinguishing the lights he'd just lit, when dawn began to lighten the gray of their world, he felt ill with apprehension. When Danny turned up to collect him, the Barman's face pallid and drawn in the sooty light, he felt ready almost to back out.

Then he thought of Olivia and her pain.

"Ye ready for this?" Danny asked.

Benton stuffed his equipment into his kit bag even as Andy turned up, moving like a shadow.

"He'll be comin' down the street soon," Benton said, referring to the Cat. "Any minute now. Ye have that blanket?"

Danny indicated that he did, folded beneath one arm.

"Let's stand up against them buildin's," Andy whispered, "and wait."

They did. The rain fell softly and Benton could hear his companions breathing, puffing out steam as if they were the mechanicals.

Footsteps sounded down the street.

"Here he comes."

Benton half hoped it would be someone else, not the Cat in question. Then he wouldn't have to go through with this. Not this morning.

But the now-familiar figure came in sight. Alone and moving steadily down the cobbles, stepping with dainty care through the mud.

He stood about chin-high to Benton, perhaps ear-height to his two companions, and even in the dim light Benton could see he was richly dressed, wearing heeled boots and a fine cloak over what was no doubt a satin suit. He carried the folded robe and a cane, which tap-tapped as he approached.

The breath nearly seized in Benton's lungs. It would be so easy to just let him pass by.

But Danny grunted, "Now," and Benton leaped forward with his two fellows, completely forgetting one of his greatest concerns, whether there was anyone else on the street to see them.

They surrounded the Cat, who gave a kind of steamy huff of surprise or outrage and Danny threw the blanket over him. All three of them grabbed hold tight.

Benton rarely touched a mechanical, having no cause in the normal course of life. They held themselves aloof and apart from humans. He did not expect the slender body to be so strong, though he should have, knowing the damage the Ferret had done to Olivia.

Now the figure in their arms, even though wrapped in the blanket, fought hard. Unnaturally strong it was, beneath the fur and fine clothing. Andy grunted again as he was kicked by a steel-framed knee. A claw got loose and raked Benton's side, tearing cloth and flesh.

"Hold 'im. Get 'im into the shadows!"

An imperative. A carriage could appear at any moment or a pair of Dogs on patrol. They wrestled the struggling mechanical into a nearby alley, and it took the combined strength of all three of them.

"Ugh!" Danny cried. "Sit on him, Benny. Use your weight."

Benton did, smashing the Cat down onto the muddy bricks of the alley, but the mechanical heaved beneath him and gave off a yowling that must be audible for blocks.

"Get off me! Let me go, scum! I demand you release me."

"What do we do?" gasped Andy, trying to hold their victim down and completely panicked.

"Find the switch," Danny growled. "Where Madam said."

"Can't see. It's too dark. The damn thing's under his clothes. We need light."

"Drag him to the cellar."

They never thought it would be so difficult, or so loud. Any blows they rained upon the shrouded figure had no effect, and he continued to yowl until Danny pressed the fabric of the rough blanket into his mouth.

The mechanical body felt hot beneath Benton's hands and terror nearly closed his throat.

But they got their victim to the cellar, that location chosen partly because it was not far, where others of the group waited. It took five of them to carry the struggling Cat down the stairs to where they threw him down and stared at each other.

"By God!" one of them said.

"Sammy, ye guard the door."

"On it."

One man slipped outside. Another stood at the top of the stairs. The Cat lay on its back on the stone floor, still wrapped in the blanket.

"Let's see what we've got," said Billy.

"Wait." Danny. "I'm not sure whether it saw us. As soon as ye uncover it—"

"It will be able to identify us."

"Leave its head wrapped. We need to find that switch."

They bundled the cloth around the victim's head, and Benton sat on it. A feeling of unreality had now found him, a certainty that none of this could truly be happening, that they hadn't actually followed through with their wild scheme, and didn't have a Cat in their hands.

His heart near pounded from his chest as he kept their victim down using all his weight, and the others tore open its clothing, rough in their haste, searching. *Searching.*

A fine, lustrous dark blue cloak now ruined with mud. Mustard-colored pantaloons beneath, and a striped gold-on-white waistcoat. All ripped away even as the Cat growled and snarled. Danny held one arm and someone else the other so the Cat couldn't claw them.

Beneath the clothing, luxuriant fur. The Cat was a longhair, gray with white on his chest and belly. Somewhere in all that fur—

What if Gloria was wrong? What if she'd been maddened, after all, by her suffering? What if they did not find the switch where she said, just in a place most impossible to reach?

"Is it there?" he gasped.

Danny reached between the Cat's legs, high up on one thigh. His fingers plowed through the fur there. "Nothin'. Oh, God, there's nothin'."

"It was the other leg," Benton said. "The right one."

195

"Oh." More fumbling. A sob came from Danny, torn out of him, and the Cat went suddenly limp.

The cellar became absolutely quiet, not a sound.

Someone sobbed and swiftly muffled it.

Hoarse breathing commenced in the room.

"There. She was right. It's there." Danny growled much as the Cat had. The Cat which now lay still and inoperative.

Benton crawled off its head.

"Let's take a look," Andy said.

They unwound the blanket from the mechanical's head. The fur there lay mussed, a condition Benton would bet rarely afflicted the creature. He'd had a monocle, which lay broken. His eyes, tawny gold in contrast to his gray fur, were wide open, but he could not see them.

Still, it was horribly disconcerting.

"It worked," said Andy again. "He's shut down."

A major victory, and they took turns reveling in it, poking at the creature and shaking it. The body felt hot, for the fire in its chest still burned. Only the gears that propelled its limbs and piped steam throughout it had ceased.

Each of them took a turn locating the switch there between its thighs, high on the inside of the right leg, a location easy for the mechanical to guard. No ordinary switch, it lay deep in the fur and had to be depressed with some force, to function.

"What do we do with him now?" Marty asked.

"Ye know what we do. Turn him back on. Put him back on the street," Benton answered. That had been the plan.

"But what if he's seen us? And—we've said each

other's names. He'll have heard."

Sammy had come tiptoeing back down the stairs. They stood in a circle staring at the Cat.

"That was the plan," Benton said woodenly.

"Yes, but—wouldn't it be safer to destroy him?" Danny suggested.

"Destroy him?"

"Smash him to pieces. Throw the pieces in the river. That way he can't ever identify us."

"And when he goes missin'? What then?"

Another silence fell.

"They won't find him, if he's in the river."

"There'll be an awful hue and cry."

"He'll remember he was grabbed, if we turn him back on. There'll be a hue and cry anyway."

"If he didn't see us—"

"What if he did? Or heard our names?"

They struggled over it, standing there around the object that was no more than steel and gears and fur.

"That wasn't the plan," Benton persisted. Sure, he understood the impulse to destroy the thing now that they had it in their hands, or at their feet. It belonged to the class determined to keep them down, and never had they possessed such an opportunity.

He whispered, "He's probably a justice at the Council. Of high command."

"Or a worker there, shufflin' papers."

"Even so."

"He had that robe. We dropped it someplace."

"And his cane."

"We'll have to go back and find those. Make sure they go into the river with him."

"We're doin' that, then?"

Someone lashed out and kicked the Cat. Benton was never sure who. The blow, delivered by a broken-down boot, made an odd thud combined with a clang.

They were metal, after all.

What followed was not civilized and barely human. They kicked the mechanical apart, and Benton participated despite himself. He did it for Olivia because she'd also been kicked, and out of fear of discovery and a kind of crowd-madness. Even while it was happening, he felt ashamed of it.

The Cat came to pieces. Its fire went out with a smudge and the hot water spilled forth from its boiler. The fur covering split and the parts shattered, rods and gears, levers and piping.

The thing, despite its airs and attitude, was just so much metal. Components.

Maybe that was what they needed to see, these men who were no better than their fellows, and no braver in the end even though they understood this scheme.

"Well," Danny said at last, when nothing more than a heap of rubble and fur lay at their feet, "Madam Gloria was right. I guess now we know she was able to hang onto those memories after all."

Marty said, "I suggest we elect her our leader. Any woman—" he corrected himself— "any*body* with that kind of courage should stand at our head."

"Agreed. First we have to get rid of all this. Find the robe and the cane. Let's make a pile."

"Several piles," Benton corrected, "and we'll take them separately to the river." Some sanity was seeping back in. "But don't miss a scrap."

They worked diligently and Benton focused on the fact that perhaps the destruction of this unit was inevitable. Men kept down so long, terrified and frustrated, could not be expected to release their victim whole.

"What d'ye think the Cats will do," Andy asked, "when this one doesn't turn up for its post?"

"Start an investigation. Send out the Dogs and possibly the Wolves. Trace his route." Danny looked at them. "His route leads through us."

Benton's guts tightened in apprehension. Would he be suspected? Questioned?

Did he have the courage he would need?

Chapter Nineteen

The next meeting convened three days later. By then, word of what had happened flew far and wide, and when they gathered at a new site, far away from their usual patch, their numbers had increased still farther. They fair burst the little room behind a tailor's shop.

Sunday had come and gone. Olivia and Benton spent it in bed together, not making love, for she wasn't yet ready for that, but just holding each other, talking in murmurs. Speculating. Not really expressing their fears, which remained legion.

No one appeared to be looking for the missing Cat, which of itself seemed suspicious.

Cats were meticulous and unlikely to write off the absence of one of their number. On his rounds, Benton had noticed no increase in the patrols, though his uneasiness made him feel as if those who were out and about eyed him with increased suspicion.

Not a word appeared in the broadsheets concerning the Cat's disappearance.

That was one of the first matters brought up at the meeting. No one there believed the disappearance had escaped notice, and so it seemed the Police must be investigating in secret.

"Which means," Danny declared, "they do not want us to know what they suspect."

"Which means," Freddie chimed in, "they may well

200

suspect us."

"Us?"

"Humans, I mean. That is, they don't suspect this Cat met with an accident. Was it hit by a carriage or did it meet with a mechanical failure along the way?"

"If it had, they'd have found him, or parts of him. The lot who captured him—" the speaker, an older man named Jeffy, looked at Benton and the others, "put every bit of him in the river."

"Bits of him may turn up yet, then," cried a woman. "That river throws things up all the time."

Gloria spoke. The others all listened to her respectfully, since she'd been elected their leader. "I think it's safe to say if anyone had seen anythin' durin' the capture, the Cats or Dogs—or Wolves—would have questioned ye immediately. They're straightforward that way. I believe the fact that they're keepin' the disappearance quiet means they're stymied at the moment, and don't want to admit it. They don't want word to get out so that those like us—" she gave a disconcerting, sharp smile—"will get ideas and do it again."

Danny asked her respectfully, "Will we do it again, Madame Gloria?"

"Yes, of course. But we'll be clever about it. No leapin' out upon our prey like savages. We'll lure them to us, instead."

Everyone there stared, some with apprehension and some with eagerness. The hate in the room became palpable.

"How do we lure them?" Danny asked.

Gloria's gaze moved to Olivia. "I've been told that in a past meetin', before I left the jail, there was discussion of how the Lord High built certain authentic characteristics into his creations. Wolves can be fierce, Racoons clever. Cats can be aloof—and curious. I believe we should use that curiosity against them."

"How?" Several voices around the circular room asked the question.

"What do cats abhor?" Gloria asked.

"Us."

"Defiance."

"Water."

Beside Benton, Olivia spoke up. "Mice."

Gloria pointed a finger at her. "Exactly."

"But," said a woman, bewildered, "they live with House Mice in their homes."

"Those are mechanical mice. I'm speakin' of the real thing."

"There are no real mice," a man objected, "and no real critters of any kind left in the world. Isn't that why the Lord High created his mechanical ones?"

"Yes. But what if word spread that a number of actual mice had survived and turned up? Would the Cats be able to resist findin' out?"

Benton snapped his fingers. "Mouse sightin's. Around the City."

"In isolated places," Gloria agreed.

"Won't the Cats just send out Dog Patrols to investigate?"

"They might," Gloria agreed. "But I think that, bein' Cats, they'll want to see for themselves."

A silence, deep and intense, fell while everyone thought about that.

"I reckon it could work," Danny said.

"It's worth a try," Gloria told him. "But listen to me.

The Cats that are lured to the chosen locations must only be shut off. They can't be destroyed. We want the Lord High to know we are onto his secret. That we can shut down his Cats any time we please."

"Why not just smash them all?"

"Because we have to live in this City, and that means we'll need to negotiate a way forward. A peace."

Several people snorted.

"If we go about smashin' and destroyin' units like vigilantes, we'll all be put in prison, and nothin' will ever change for the better."

Benton said, "We may be put in prison anyway."

"We might. If we're caught. That is why anyone who's not sure about takin' the risk should back out now. We'll form an elite group of those who wish to move forward. All I ask from the rest of ye is to keep silent."

But she had given them something they'd never had before—hope. Benton doubted there would be many who wanted to back out.

Olivia said, "Madam Gloria, as soon as we start shuttin' down the first Cats, won't the Lord High know from whence came our information? Surely he'll suspect ye. Ye'll be at the greatest risk of all."

"Yes. He'll have to tumble to the fact that my mind wasn't completely wiped after all when I was released. I suppose I'll have to go into hidin'."

"We'll pass ye around the City," a man said, "from one of us to the next, not long in one place at a time."

"That might work." Gloria gazed about the room. "But it shares the risk around among any who agree to help me."

"It shares the trust also," Benton said. "Ye'll have to trust all of us."

Gloria gazed from face to face. She looked so small and frail standing there with her pinched face and shorn head and her great burning eyes. Quite simply she said, "I do. I trust each of ye."

They swelled with pride. These people who had been kept down so long, despised, and denied a say in their own lives, everything from their jobs to where they lived being assigned.

Danny drew himself up and spoke for all of them. "Madam Gloria, I would sooner die than betray ye."

Spirit, Benton thought. That was what she had gifted all of them. And so, to betray her would be to betray their own souls.

"So," Gloria tipped up her chin, "when do we begin?"

****

It was agreed that the undertaking would begin immediately with the spreading of rumors. Whispers out on the street that were sure to come to the Cats' ears sooner rather than later. Organic mice had been sighted. They were infesting cellars and back alleys. Byways.

Isolated places.

"We'll have only so long," Marty pointed out, "before it comes to the Lord High's ears and he shuts it down. Forbids his Cats from investigatin' reports of mice."

"They still may not be able to resist," someone pointed out. "Ye remember the old sayin', curiosity killed the cat."

"Just so." Gloria gave another sharp smile. "We shall have to spread our sightin's across the City, lure as many Cats as possible before the Lord High gets onto us."

"The Cats will see us, won't they? When they turn up all curious at the sites of the reports?"

"Yes. That is why ye must hide your faces—muffle them in scarves. They'll know we're human, but not which humans."

Olivia asked, "What if the Lord High decides to punish all of us? O make examples of some?"

"He may well do that once he learns that his secret is out. That is why I say to ye again, back out now if ye don't wish to share the risk."

"We'll share the risk," Danny declared, "just as we share bein' under their thumbs. I have only one question, Madam Gloria."

"What's that?"

"Do ye think all the mechanicals have an off switch in the same place?"

"Who knows, Danny? I saw only the plans—the blueprint—for the Cat. But I do not think it would be an erroneous assumption."

"So," said a big man, not without relish," once we take care of the Cats, we'll have to make another capture, right? And find out, say, about the Dogs."

They gazed at one another uncertainly.

"Unless," ventured a woman, "the Lord High decides to make alterations so we can't shut them off."

"He may well try," said another man, "but he can't change all of them at once, or very quickly."

"Let's take it one step at a time," Gloria told them. "The rumors first. To the resistance!"

"To the resistance!"

****

It was not deemed necessary for Gloria to abandon her room at once, so Olivia accompanied her back there after the meeting, Benton having to begin his rounds.

"Are ye sure ye'll be all right here?" she asked Gloria when they reached the place. "Would ye like me to stay the night?"

"No reason for me to suppose I'm in danger yet," Gloria declared calmly.

"But—later. Once we begin shuttin' down the Cats and the Lord High figures out ye must be the one spreadin' the information—"

"Then I'll be in danger, yes. I don't doubt he'll send the Grey Guard out after me."

Olivia shivered. She feared the Grey Guard on a visceral level. "D'ye think he'll figure it out?"

"Oh, yes, and it won't take him long. He's a genius, after all." Her dark gaze met Olivia's. "I figure my life will be forfeit. No matter how the members of the group try to protect me, the Grey Guard will take me down. But I believe it's worth it. I might have died back there on the table durin' torture. They might have eliminated me after. At least this way, I'll accomplish somethin' before I die."

"Ye've lit a fire, and no mistake."

"The only thing that worries me is, if they trace my path, blame may fall on those who helped me. Ye, for instance. Since this is your room, I'll clear out soon and maybe they won't know I stayed here."

"I think everyone is willin' to take their chances."

"Ye say that now." Horror glinted in Gloria's eyes. "I know what may follow."

"Yes." Olivia doubted she'd be very good at withstanding torment.

"Gloria, why do ye think the Lord High sided with animals after the Great Killing and abandoned his fellow man?"

"He's a genius, as everyone says, and from what I glimpsed of him, one teeterin' on an edge between brilliance and madness. I suspect he was somethin' of a recluse before all this happened. Perhaps denigrated by the humans in his life."

"And now we're payin' the price for how other humans treated him?"

"The sins of the fathers, and all that. Try not to worry."

"Impossible."

"Any of us lost will be considered heroes."

Yes, Olivia thought. Dead ones.

****

The rumors spread the way rumors tend to do, in whispers along the streets and back alleys and in the taverns. Humans within earshot of any Cats while exchanging the words made sure to stop talking—but not too soon.

For days it was difficult to tell whether the effort was succeeding. Cats continued to drive out in their fancy carriages and to stroll in their finery. No one seemed to be paying particular attention to the nonsense the humans might be spouting.

The first hint that they did pay attention appeared in a very small article in one of the broadsheets, entitled, "Do Organic Mice Exist?"

The broadsheets were intended for the benefit and entertainment of the mechanicals. Most humans were assumed to be unable to read, whereas all mechanicals were programmed with the ability.

In truth, more than a few humans had picked up the skill to some degree and many of those perused the broadsheets.

Benton brought a copy of the one in question home to Olivia, and they puzzled it out together.

"It doesn't say much, does it?" Olivia faltered. "Only a few lines."

"Yes." Benton leaned in so close, his head almost touched hers. "But I think they're significant lines, don't ye?"

Olivia ran a finger under the print. *Do Organic Mice Exist? Reports of rodents being sighted in the City must be either greatly exaggerated or entirely false. A living, non-mechanical mouse has not been observed in nearly some thirty years. Cats at the Council have ordered an investigation.*

"I think that's the important point, don't ye? That last line. The rumors have reached the right ears and they mean to pursue the matter."

Of course they did, Olivia thought. Being Cats, how could they resist?

"But," she said, "What if they assign the Wolves to investigate? We don't know but that the Wolves are constructed entirely differently, and if anyone tries to fall upon them—"

She hoped that would not be Benton. She prayed it wouldn't, even though she would have said she'd long since given up praying.

She feared it would.

He huffed out a breath. "That would be unfortunate."

"It would." The Wolves would arrest on the spot anyone they saw or, at the very least, remember their faces and track them down later.

"Benton, maybe we shouldn't pursue this. Maybe

we should back out. It's too dangerous."

"Think of the Ferrets," he said and his words were hard, even though his hand on her belly was infinitely gentle. The place where their child just may have been conceived.

"Olivia, we can't go on like this—like craven cowards afraid to raise our heads to the sky." He tugged her around to meet his gaze. "If we're ever to have a life, if our children are, we must try to break free."

"But I love ye." Her lips trembled. "And I can't bear to lose ye."

His gaze softened. "Ye won't."

"Can ye promise that to me?"

He began to shake his head and then hesitated. "Yes, I can. Because I believe the things we love are always with us. I'm part of ye now, as ye're part of me. We'll always be together in spirit."

"That's not what I meant."

"It's what I can offer ye, darlin'."

She went into his arms and they clung together, and despite his bright and loving words, fear flooded Olivia's mind. Precious to her he was, from his steady eyes to the hairs that grew upon his chest. She'd never understood what love could be till she knew him, and now she was in too deep to save her heart.

"Olivia, listen to me." He tipped her face up, fingers beneath her chin. "It will be worth it even if we don't succeed. It's a matter of standin' up for ourselves. Of bein' human."

"I'm so afraid."

"Fear is part of bein' human too. But, Olivia, don't ask me to go through the years ahead knowin' I can't protect ye. It's more than I can bear."

He kissed her and she felt it all. His desire to protect her, his need to fight for her, and the love. Most of all, the love.

And yet she prayed feverishly in her mind, please, *please don't let it be him.*

## Chapter Twenty

Reports began coming in from all over the City. Cats were being waylaid, caught alone in isolated places, wrapped in cloaks or blankets and summarily shut down. The first accounts came to Olivia's ears during the course of her work day when she overheard two House Mice whispering about it in the Grey Guard's kitchen. Their high, agitated squeaks did not escape her attention.

"None of them have been damaged. Just shut off." The horror inherent in that second statement made Olivia stop scrubbing and sit up. Odd to think mechanicals experienced horror. But if Cats experienced curiosity— and events proved they must—then a creature for eons hunted by everything from hawks to felines might know a thing or two about the terror of the prey.

"And none of them has seen their assailants."

Due to the practice of swaddling them first—both a precaution against being glimpsed and an attempt to keep from feeling their claws.

"They're just left there. Switched off."

"Then they can be switched on again."

"Yesss. But I heard from Mistress—well, I overheard—that some of them have gaps in their memory, after."

"From being shut off."

"Yesss. So unless whoever is doing this is caught in the act—"

*No, please*. Precisely what Olivia dreaded. For despite her wishes, despite his promises and her desperate prayers, Benton did make up a member of the squads who waylaid the Cats.

Cats who fell victim to their own curiosity. For they continued to investigate the supposed rodent sightings, even when they knew the danger.

The nature of a creature, be it human or mechanical, held true, or so it seemed.

Olivia had fallen into the habit of spending her evenings, the time after Benton went to work, with Gloria. Often she couldn't sleep and found a measure of comfort in the woman's stoical demeanor.

"The Lord High will definitely be aware of what's happenin'," she told Gloria the evening after she overheard the House Mice's conversation.

"Oh, indeed, he will."

"How can ye be so calm, knowin' he'll figure out where we got the information? When he comes after ye. Indeed, ye should not stay here. Too many people know where ye are. If he puts the Grey Guard into action…"

"He will."

"And if he captures and tortures the wrong human—"

"They'll talk, yes. They'll tell whatever they know."

"So, Gloria, ye need to hide. Put the plan we made into effect. If we pass ye from place to place around the City—"

"I've been thinkin' about that."

Gloria did a lot of thinking, as Olivia well knew. In variance with her frail, ravaged body, her mind was afire and frequently plotting. "It might be better if I gave myself up."

"What?" Olivia turned and stared at her friend. For indeed, that was what Gloria had become. "No."

"When ye consider on it—"

"Why *would* ye consider it? Ye can't. Ye be our leader. Our hope." Until she spoke the words, Olivia did not realize how true they were.

Slowly, Gloria shook her head. "I may have helped set things in motion, but the lot of ye are off and runnin' now. If the Lord High knows it's I who leaked the information and if he has me in his hands, he won't pursue the rest of ye so hard, will he? Oh, he might want retribution for the attacks, but he'll have the true miscreant in his hands."

Olivia perched on the bed beside Gloria. "Ye can't go back into that. Not—not knowin' what they will do to ye."

"Don't worry. I won't give the rest of ye away. I know what I can endure. I'll die before he breaks me."

"I don't want ye to die! I don't want ye to sacrifice yourself and become a martyr."

"It might be the best use I can make of myself now. I'll never recover physically; that's somethin' I've realized."

"That doesn't matter. We need ye."

"Ye'll find other heroes, some of them unexpected, perhaps. That Danny, now—" Gloria broke off. "Here, Olivia, don't cry."

"I'm not."

"Ye are. Come, ye're stronger than that. Remember we met at one of the worst places on earth, and I know ye."

Olivia swiped at her wet cheeks. "It's not fair. Ye've suffered enough. More than any one person should."

"Life is not fair. If we know anythin', it's that. We can attempt to make it a little more so. I can, by givin' myself up."

Olivia contemplated it and suddenly understood the frustration that had beset Benton all this while, the helpless desire to protect. She wanted to protect Gloria and did not know how.

Could they, the members of the resistance, hide her somewhere? Hold her against her will, maybe, so she couldn't turn herself in?

"But we need ye," she repeated. "We need your wisdom and your strength."

"I appreciate that, Olivia. But I suggest what ye don't need is the whole City mobilized against ye, as the Lord High searches for me."

"He'll destroy ye, this time." He would burn her brain into oblivion, even if he did not kill her. "Make certain ye cannot think to threaten him and his again."

"I know it. I'm willin'."

Olivia could not imagine such courage.

"Please," she begged, "don't do anythin' hasty. Let us discuss it with the others."

"All right. We'll do that," Gloria agreed. But the concession came too easily and Olivia did not believe her. Not quite.

\*\*\*\*

The notice appeared on the front of the next day's broadsheet in bold type.

*Warning.*

*No Cat is to pursue the hunt for rodents no matter from whence the report issues. There are no living rodents, and such reports are false rumors meant to lead Cats into danger. Do not heed them.*

Benton saw it on his way to work that Wednesday evening, the sheets on the street corner in a dispenser safe from the rain. He paused long enough to peruse it and stepped away pretending to adjust his pack while watching the Cats on the street dispense copies for themselves.

What would this do to their scheme? They were in fact supposed to congregate that night on the wharf that fronted the river, where not mice but rats had supposedly been sighted.

Most of the members of his route and the adjacent routes were now members of the resistance. They'd developed a system of covering for each other while they went off in small squads to do their business, often meeting with other resistance members, like Danny Barman, on the way. They'd become swift and effective in their job. But with increased numbers of attackers, as the papers called them, the Dogs and undoubtedly the Wolves were also out in increased numbers. It grew dangerous.

This night, as he passed along word of the notice, he thought of Olivia. On some level, she remained always in his mind, but now he acknowledged how perilous their situation became.

If he got picked up—and each foray increased the risk that he would—what would it do to her? Should he make an effort to call a halt to what they were doing?

Could he call a halt, if he tried? The squads out pursuing lone Cats had very nearly run wild. Oh, they were still careful, knowing what was at stake, but after being powerless so long, the ability to shut down their tormentors had pretty much gone to their heads. Even his? Well, by and large he considered himself levelheaded, but there was a fierce and savage satisfaction in shutting one of those mechanicals down. Of having the unit in his power, knowing he could destroy it if he wanted to. Could destroy dozens of them. Indeed, a couple of squads—not his—had given in to temptation and done just that.

He asked himself constantly what he would do if one of the Cats they waylaid saw him before they'd shut it down. Would he give in and destroy it so it couldn't give him away?

To protect Olivia, who needed him, he might.

Such thoughts still dominated his mind when he met up with his fellows on the wharf side. They disappeared into the shadows while he told them about the broadsheet.

"A watershed moment," whispered Danny, who had joined them. "Will the Cats obey that notice? Or will curiosity truly get the better of them?"

"They're mechanicals," Andy hissed back. "Not real cats. They can be only so curious."

"Even so—"

They shut up then because footsteps echoed down the wharf side. Someone approached. Might be a Dog Patrol. Any random mechanical.

But no—a single Cat came into view. He might have been a professional by day, employed in some government position. Now he was a Tom out on the prowl and unable to resist the lure of actual rodents that he might pursue.

Someone in the little knot of Lightmen—and a single Barman—gave a grunt.

*Wait till he comes closer*, Benton thought. *Wait*.

The Cat slowed his pace—perhaps looking for the

purported rodents—and they got a good look at him in the light of one of the few overhead lamps here. He was clad like one of the dandies—like a Fox, more than a Cat—with close-fitting pantaloons and high-heeled shoes, a satin waistcoat and velvet cape. His black-and-white fur gleamed, and his eyes—

Benton got only a glimpse of them before the blanket enfolded the mechanical and they wrestled him down.

That was the moment everything went wrong.

The Cat fought harder than most of the units they had disabled. He yowled and struggled in their grip. A claw came out and caught Benton on the jaw.

As they struggled to pin him down and shut him off, more footsteps sounded from the opposite direction. A pair of Dogs came racing in.

Someone in their group hollered. Someone else succeeded in finding the switch at the Cat's groin, and he went still. The Dogs came on, waving their batons and growling horrifically.

Somebody yelled, "Run!"

There was no time. The Dogs, a pair of Dobermans, were already upon then, snarling. Benton caught a flash of them in their blue uniforms before the batons began swinging, each blow coaxing a grunt from its human recipient.

Benton rolled and ducked away. He could feel blood welling from the furrows the Cat had left on his jaw and he didn't want either of the Dogs to get a good look at him. They were barking, which would call other Police, and if the humans didn't escape now they would not have a chance.

That was when he scrambled up and met the stare of

one Doberman Police officer. The mechanical was in mid-bark, his mouth open and all his razor teeth on display when their gazes met.

Benton could almost see the mechanical catch his likeness and store it in his mind.

He had a split second then to decide what to do. Instinct made him dive for the Doberman, catch it around the knees and take it down. Confusion reigned—his companions still taking blows from the other Doberman. Some had already fled.

"Help me, help me," Benton cried, tearing at his victim's clothing. It was Danny who surged up and pinned the Doberman down for a breathless moment while Benton reached inside the unit's clothing, groping obscenely. Groping.

Would the switch be there? Had the Lord High created all his animals equally?

His fumbling fingers plowed through fur. Met with metal. Structural metal, not a switch. Then he found it, the tiny recessed button that must be pushed.

The Doberman went abruptly still. Danny lifted his head and exchanged a single, incredulous look with Benton before throwing himself into the fray against the second police dog.

"There's a switch. A switch! Same place!"

Benton struggled to his feet, looking down at the Doberman. When the Lord High switched it back on, would it remember him? Would he be recorded in its artificial intelligence or would there be a blank in the unit's memory?

"We're makin' too much noise," someone said just before the second Doberman shut down. "Quick, let's get out of here."

Benton continued eyeing the unit at his feet. He had to make sure, for Olivia's sake, if not his own.

"Let's destroy them," he said.

"No. We haven't been—"

"They saw us."

"Benny's right. They did see us."

"But the penalty for destroyin' 'em will be higher than just for shuttin' 'em down."

"Penalty's goin' to be high either way." It was Danny, breathless. "But we've learned somethin' valuable tonight. Worth it."

Those left on the wharf grunted assent.

"Let's throw 'em in the water."

They did, sliding the mechanicals in carefully so there was no splash. Then they melted away through the shadows, leaving only the Cat lying behind.

Benton returned to his route. But his hands continued to shake so he could barely do his work.

Chapter Twenty-One

"Hold still, Benton, please."

Olivia murmured the entreaty as she leaned close and dabbed at the ugly furrows on the left side of Benton's jaw. Four of them there were, and cut deep. They had partially closed over while he finished his night's work and oozed but slowly now, thick, dark blood that Olivia sought to wipe away as gently as possible.

She'd been stunned when he came home, catching her before she left for her day's work. Horrified. But not surprised.

Down at the root of her soul, she had known something like this would happen. It had been a matter of time. From here, it could only get worse.

Her eyes met his where she hunched beside him on the edge of the bed, the room affording no other place, mere inches apart.

"Ye say he saw ye?"

"Yes. One of the Dobermans did."

Olivia struggled not to let her panic show. He did not need that reaction on top of everything else.

"But not the Cat? Or the other police officer?"

"I don't think so. We put both Dobermans in the river. If they stay down long enough, the water may corrode them so—"

"So he—the Lord High—can't retrieve a

description?"

"Yes."

"Oh, Benton."

"I know. But they—the Dobermans—came out of nowhere. We knew the patrols had been increased, but we thought all was clear."

Olivia said nothing, though her thoughts raced.

"If they don't surface, it's possible no one will know they were there. The Cat was already shut off."

"Yes, but surely they have to report somewhere? They'll be missed."

"No way to tell who tossed them in the river. Hopefully."

Olivia found it difficult to hope.

"This is goin' to leave a row of scars." She told him. "Like a brand of your guilt."

"I'll stop shavin' and let my beard grow." He gazed into her eyes. "Will ye still love me with a beard?"

For answer, she kissed him. "Only till forever. Ye'd better grow that beard fast. Because they'll be lookin'."

She did not tell him about the conversation she'd had with Gloria, and the woman's desire to sacrifice herself.

"As Danny said, though, we discovered somethin' important last night. Dogs have a kill switch in the same location as the Cats. That means—"

"All the different mechanicals might."

"Yes. It makes sense, since it's an easy spot for a mechanical to protect."

Olivia nodded.

"I suppose there'll have to be more captures, to be certain of it."

"If so, I don't want ye in on it. Hear me, Benton?

221

"I hear ye."

"Ye've done enough for the time bein'. Ye need to lie low. If those Dobermans surface—" She didn't complete the thought, didn't have to.

"I should get to work." She put aside the basin and bandages. "Promise ye'll stay here today. I'll see ye after I complete my houses."

"I promise."

She kissed him again, hard and quick, considered trying to tell him what he meant to her and gave it up. He didn't need the pressure. Besides, there were no words.

She remained on pins and needles all day, doing her best to overhear any household conversations, but they were surprisingly few. She went home through a downpour to find Benton still sleeping, the raked side of his face turned uppermost from the pillow. She supposed she'd need to wake him soon so he could prepare for work. She decided to crawl into bed with him instead.

The feel of cold, damp flesh against his warm skin awakened him and he drew her in. It was the first time they'd made love since her injury, and when he would have withdrawn before climaxing, she locked her heels behind him and held him in.

"Olivia," he said after. "Are ye sure?"

"Yes." Life was precious and perilous. She wanted all of him she could have, whatever the consequences.

\*\*\*\*

It took five days for one of the Dobermans to be found, after pieces of him surfaced. Frogmen—quite literally Frogs—were sent down to investigate, and the remnants of both units were brought up.

As the broadsheets reported, both were heavily corroded. The water in the river was not mere water.

Since the worldwide disasters that prompted the Great Killing, there were chemicals and residue that could destroy a man—or apparently a mechanized Dog.

As the broadsheet reported, the retrieved pieces of the Dobermans were taken to the palace to be sorted and, if possible, repaired.

A meeting was convened once more up above the tavern. It felt strange having more people crowded into the upper room than were down at the bar, for humans still kept off the streets, for the most part, and out of the taverns.

They discussed their situation with a new, perilous honesty. They had changed, so Olivia could not help but think, from the somewhat bumbling group they had once been. Fate had put much upon them, and glancing around the room she realized how they held one another's safety in their hands.

If the Lord High learned something of value from the salvaged Dobermans, or if he decided to randomly question people for information, could these individuals hold strong?

She looked at Benton, who sat with the air of quiet he so often assumed, that covered a morass of emotions inside. Over the past five days, his beard had grown in and now made a fuzz surrounding the deeply grooved wounds on his jaw. But it would not be difficult for the authorities to see through that, should suspicion fall upon him. And her heart twisted with fearful love.

Her world, so it seemed, was made up of mud, and debt, the gears of those who stood against them, of loss and—yes—its flip side, love.

Those present debated the condition of the Dobermans when they came out of the water, how even the Frogmen had needed to don protective suits before venturing into the river. Surely conditions would protect them from discovery.

"And yet," said Gloria, who had insisted on attending the meeting, "we cannot forget the Lord High's brilliance. He created the artificial intelligence that he will now plumb. I would not wish for ye to grow overconfident. Every step we take is rife with risk, though unquestionably necessary."

Everyone there looked to her with complete attention. From a small, frail woman she had without a doubt become their guiding star.

Now she got to her feet and stepped to the head of the room.

"We have, as has been stated, discovered somethin' immeasurably important, proof that the Dobermans, and no doubt the rest of the Dogs, have the same kill switch as the Cats we've handled. There will be no need to capture or harass any more Cats, though—" she gave a wry smile—"we have learned somethin' important there also, have we not? That despite the fact that they are mechanical, they are indeed still curious. They could not resist the lure we set for them, just like the true cats of old. That, my friends, is a weapon, when we have precious few.

"And it will doubtless be true of the other mechanicals also. The Lord High will have built a characteristic into each of them. To use it to our advantage, we need only discover the nature of each animal's, well, nature."

"Dogs used to be man's best friend," said a woman. "Not now."

"No, not now," Gloria agreed. "Yet perhaps loyalty

might be their weakness, or duty. Devotion. And Foxes—perhaps their devious natures. Wolves—their efficient ferocity. It will be up to ye to uncover those traits which may mean much to ye in the future. As for me—" Gloria paused and gazed around the small, packed room. "I will not be with ye. I have decided to hand myself in to the authorities. To take the blame for the secret that has been leaked."

For one moment, the only sound was that of the rain, the eternal rain, crashing onto the roof. Then came the outcry of protest and objection. She should not. She could not.

Gloria stood, a small, pitiable figure that was somehow far from pitiable, and let it wash over her, saying nothing till they quieted, when she spoke again.

"My friends—I am touched by your desire to protect me." Her voice broke. "But the crime in question was in fact mine."

"And ye've paid for it. By God, ye've paid." It was Danny Barman who spoke. Olivia was surprised and a little shocked to see a bright glow of love in the philanderer's eyes when he gazed at Gloria.

Murmurs of agreement sounded all over the room.

Gloria shook her head. "If the Lord High gets any information from the Dobermans, he will not stop until he finds the sources. The best way I can protect all of ye and the movement is to turn myself in as that source."

"Will the Lord High believe ye?" a woman asked. "Look at the state of ye!"

"I can be convincin'."

"He'll torture ye," Danny said hoarsely, "to learn other names."

"Yes, no doubt. I will not betray ye."

"And," it was Benton who spoke fiercely, "we will not betray ye either. Or each other. But we won't see ye turn yourself in."

"Let me do this," Gloria said. "It is the best use ye can make of me."

"It is not!" Danny roared. "Our best use is to have ye as our leader. I say we vote on the matter, as people used to do. All those in favor of protectin' Madam Gloria, protectin' her even from herself if we have to, say aye."

A thunder of *ayes* shook the room. When it died away, tears stood in Gloria's eyes.

"We'll move ye about the City so he can't find ye," Danny declared. "And someone always with ye, on guard." So no one could reach her, and she could not sacrifice herself. "Is everyone in?"

Another chorus, this one less violent.

Gloria held up a hand. "I will agree to this on one condition. If it comes down to ruination—if there is absolutely no other option and it looks like our movement will be destroyed—ye must then allow me to turn myself over in an effort to buy your safety."

Those in the room looked at one another uneasily. Slow nods came.

"Yes," Danny spoke for them. "But just know, Madam Gloria, there are always other options."

****

Benton and Olivia walked home slowly after the meeting, him with his arm around her. He had to report to work and they would need to part at the door of his building. For the moment, they pretended to be no more than a couple on their way back from a tavern.

"Did ye see the look in Danny's eyes?" Olivia

asked. "They way he gazed at Gloria. Do ye think he's in love with her?"

Benton contemplated the question. He would not have supposed a man of Danny's ilk who went about attempting to impregnate as many women as possible was capable of love. But then he'd once thought the same of himself, and just look at him.

"I think he may be sufferin' from a measure of hero-worship. He's never seen anyone like Gloria."

"None of us has. He took her home with him. Do ye think they'll—"

"No. I doubt she'll agree to that."

Olivia sighed. "I wish we could spend tonight together."

"So do I."

They'd reached the door of his building and turned to face each other in the pouring rain.

"Ye'll be careful out there?" At the end of the meeting it had been decided that another mechanical should be waylaid at random, just to make certain its kill switch was in the same place on all models.

Olivia peered up into Benton's face. "Promise me it won't be ye goin' out on another attack."

"I promise." He needed no further trouble for the time being.

"And promise ye'll come home early enough that we can make love before I leave for work."

Incipient delight flooded through Benton as he imagined the warmth of her, the welcoming softness. "Yes."

"Well, ye're very obligin' tonight. Kiss me."

He did, the initial press of lips on lips leading to more as she parted to him and he swept his tongue inside, the taste of her going straight to his head.

When the kiss ended, she clung to him tight. "Promise ye'll come back to me."

"I promise." Like a fool, he gave a vow he might not be able to keep.

## Chapter Twenty-Two

Halfway through the night, when Benton had got all his lamps lit and had not yet begun to extinguish them again, they met on a corner, the bunch of them, mostly all Lightmen who had fallen into the habit of checking in with one another, if only by sight. Indeed, the habit consisted of mostly brief moments, for it was raining hard, the cold drops crashing down, and no one wanted to stand out in it for long.

It had made a nightmare of the first half of the night's work. Climbing up and down the streaming poles had done a job on Benton's hands which had not fully healed, and he nearly fell twice.

They came together by what seemed like chance, and in mutual agreement the five of them stepped into the nearest alley, which lent at least marginal protection against the wet.

"Quiet tonight," said Mikey, motioning at the street. "Nobody about, not even Cats."

It was true, Benton realized. It lent an eerie feeling that had accompanied him on his rounds.

Jordie grinned, baring bad teeth. "Maybe they're all afraid of gettin' waylaid, wrapped up in a blanket, and shut off."

Upon the thought, footsteps echoed down the street beyond the alley, sounding staccato amid the rain. The Lightmen exchanged a look, and those nearest the mouth of the alley, which included Benton, peered out.

Benton expected to see a Dog patrol, for they had increased in number since the attacks began. Or perhaps a Fox all duded up in finery, for they were most likely to be out at so late an hour, alone.

Instead he saw a Racoon. He came along the street boldly. Your typical Racoon wasn't afraid of much, moving with brisk confidence. Bound on some matter of business, no doubt nefarious, since even the wealthiest Racoons—and from his clothing this one appeared very wealthy indeed—made their living from some form of theft or other.

This one wore a long, patterned cloak, the worth of which would likely keep a human's family fed for half a year or at the very least pay down his debt, and a hat with a plume at a jaunty angle to keep off the rain. His high-heeled boots, now liberally splashed with mud, made the rapid *click-clack* that had caught their attention.

Benton wondered what unfortunate human would have to clean those boots.

A few grunts marked the Racoon's progress before someone in the little knot of men said, "Let's grab him."

Benton never remembered, later, who it was that made the suggestion, though he tried, it changing his life the way it did.

*No*, he thought, but the others pressed toward the mouth of the alley to get a look.

"There's no one about," said Jordie, right in Benton's ear. "And we need to get a look at somethin' besides Cats and Dogs, to check the switch."

"No," said Benton, aloud this time.

The Racoon continued to toddle along and would soon pass them. The rest of the street appeared deserted save for the rain. Not so much as a carriage passed.

Yes, it was a good opportunity. But he had promised Olivia—

"We can check his switch," said Mikey, "and leave him here in the alley, unharmed."

"Report back to Madam Gloria," another Lightman agreed, "at the next meetin'."

Jordie began stripping off his sodden coat. "We'll wrap him in this. Drag him back here. He'll never get a glimpse of us."

"No." Benton began to say, "I promised—"

"Stay here, then," one of them told him and they rushed past him, Jordie brandishing his coat as they went.

From the mouth of the alley, Benton saw it all. The way the Racoon—a beautiful specimen now that Benton got a better look at him—shied and halted. The crowd of men descending on him the way bees might on someone who threatened their hive.

The men wrapped the Racoon in the great coat and began hauling him, struggling mightily, toward the alley. They hadn't taken five steps before a whistle sounded, cutting like a knife through the clatter of the rain.

A pair of Dogs erupted from the far end of the street. Benton's heart sank so violently, it turned him sick, and a wave of stark panic arose.

The men who clutched the Racoon froze an instant and then let go of him. The Racoon fell to the muddy cobbles.

But the men had been seen by the Dogs, who had keen sight. They scattered, even though with their packs on their backs it must be more than obvious they were Lightmen.

They had no chance to get away, for from the opposite end of the street appeared another pair of Police Dogs, and then another, seeming from nowhere. And most horrifically of all, a Grey Guard stepped from a doorway halfway down, and marched toward the now-hesitant Lightmen.

They'd been watching. And the humans hadn't even guessed they were there.

Had it in fact been a trap? Was the Racoon a decoy?

Watching, Benton shrank back from the mouth of the alley. Cries came from the men being seized by the police Dogs. His friends, captured.

Could he escape?

He glanced into the depths of the alley which wound away on a crooked path between two buildings. It probably led to Prophet Street, not part of his route. But if he could slip away, for no one had yet seen him, he might be off home to Olivia.

The only place he wanted to be.

Was it cowardly, a betrayal to abandon his fellows? Lightmen and members of the resistance. Peering out, he saw they'd all been seized, to a man.

He could not help them.

He could not run down the alley, it being narrow and dark and filled with rubble to trip him up. He edged along as quickly as he could, heading for the lighter darkness that appeared like an eye at the other end. In places, he had to angle his shoulders and go sideways. He'd nearly reached the opening, and was running the route home in his head, when the pair of Dogs stepped into view.

Blocking his escape.

He stopped dead, even before one of the Dogs barked, "Stop." He could not go back—he could still hear the commotion behind him, and anyway, the Dogs would be faster than he was. He did not think he could get past them. Even if he could, having sighted him they would run him down.

*Oh, Olivia*, he thought. *Olivia, forgive me.*

He had been foolish, and it would cost him—cost them—dear.

One of the Dogs raised his truncheon. "Step out of there, human."

He would fight. For Olivia, he would—fight to get back to her. Even if that truncheon broke his bones. But every Lightman in the City would be questioned.

And they had seen him.

"Step out, I say!"

Benton realized the command did not come from either of the Dogs. It was a sterner and colder voice entirely.

Into view at the end of the alley stepped a Wolf. He was taller than the Dogs and dressed in a long, gray cloak. In the brightness of the nearest lamp, Benton could see the long muzzle, the jaws studded with blindingly sharp, metal fangs protruding from the hood.

A Grey Guardsman.

His heart took another sickening plummet. Even if he could fight free from the Dogs, he could never outpace the Wolf, which could run like a streak.

He was fairly caught. *Oh, Olivia, forgive me.*

\*\*\*\*

The humans, the errant Lightmen, were herded into a group, Benton having been dragged around the block to join the rest of them. A veritable crowd of Police Dogs and no less than three Grey Guardsmen there were with them. A net that had closed neatly around its prey.

The Lightmen made a pitiful sight. Wet to the skin, especially Jordie, who had lost his coat, they were visibly terrified, and they drooped like cowed sheep amid a ring of sheepdogs.

In fact, several of the attendant Police *were* Sheepdogs, their eyes gleaming with the urge to crowd, to guard.

One of the Grey Guard, though not the one who had brought Benton in, addressed them.

"You are all under arrest for assaulting and attacking a Citizen of League. You will be taken to the cells below the palace and thereafter will your fates be decided."

"By trial?" asked someone anxiously.

The Guard shook his head. Even in his terror, Benton had to admit the Wolf was a magnificent creature, taller than the other two Guards and with an air of absolute authority. "No trial for the likes of you. The Lord High will himself decide your fates."

There were several gasps among the Lightmen. The Lord High?

With the air of someone who did not owe anyone an explanation, the Wolf went on, "He wishes an end to these attacks for good and all. Most of you will be sent to the mines." His icy gaze flicked toward Benton. "We need strong men there. I am certain there will be some examples made."

*Examples.*

*Executions.*

"Bring them," the Guard snapped to the Dogs.

"My wife—" one of the Lightmen bleated. "I have a wife."

"Had," the Guard corrected.

The Police Dogs herded them. When one man

whose name was Jakey broke away and tried to flee, two of the sheepdogs ran him down without difficulty and hauled him back to the Guard who'd spoken.

What happened to him, there on the spot, turned the wet cobbles from muddy to red, and put an end to anyone else trying to run.

They walked through the streets surrounded by Dogs and pelted by rain. The Dogs did not hesitate to use their truncheons liberally even though no one sought to disobey. Benton, receiving a blow to one shoulder, wondered if it had been dislocated.

It crossed his mind that so many of them—for there must be seven Lightmen or more remaining—could turn on their captors and try to shut them off. They knew where the switches were, on the Dogs at least.

But the three Grey Guards would slaughter them before they could succeed.

Eventually, the hill topped by the palace came in sight. The last time Benton had been here was when Olivia had been released. Now he would enter the bowels of the place, his very life taken out of his hands.

They stumbled, the Lightmen, up the hill. More Police Dogs waited here and more Guards. They seemed to communicate with one another by glances and soft barks. Yips.

The humans were herded inside, not to the courts but down a darkened side hallway that led to a complex set of other passageways. Endless, it seemed, and sloping ever downward.

Even if Benton could break away, he would never find his way out.

They came to a large, stone chamber that had the feel of a guardroom. A table stood at the center and half a dozen more Dogs were present. Through a far doorway, Benton could just glimpse what must be the cells.

*No. please*. He had to get word to Olivia. She would panic when he failed to return from work.

He did not want to cause her such pain. He wanted a chance to explain that he had hung back, had tried to keep his promise.

Another Grey Guard came in, as big and as grand as the one in charge. They consulted in low growls and the second Wolf left, perhaps to inform the Lord High of their capture.

He, surely, would not attend to the matter before morning.

They were herded through the far doorway and into a series of cells, one or two of them together, the rest split apart.

The cell into which Benton was prodded matched the description Olivia had given him. Malodorous, and so dark he had no hope of seeing anything.

Others were there before them—Benton heard them stir. Freddie, who stumbled in ahead of him, started to cry.

Benton wanted very much to do the same.

They stumbled to seats beside what felt like a cold, damp wall. Time dragged by. It did so as if it had broken limbs and could but inch forward. Several times Benton almost vomited. From fear, that was. He fought the sickness down, because he had no idea where to find the slop bucket Olivia had described, and did not like to further befoul the floor.

Olivia. His heart bled for her.

His thoughts raced.

What would happen to them? The mines, so the Grey Guard had said, and Benton could not make himself doubt it. Men were always needed to wrest coal, upon which their world operated, from the ground. No one ever returned from the mines. They worked till they died.

Or, the Guard had said, there would be examples made. Public executions, no doubt. Because to stop what had begun in the City, to tamp down the humans' knowledge that they could shut off the mechanicals who reigned over them, the executions would have to be public. No doubt gory. As painful as possible.

At the thought, Benton's balls tried to crawl up into his belly. If he were chosen for that—at random, most likely—could he endure the pain without shaming himself? Would Olivia be there watching?

*No, please not that.*

Could he endure without screaming or begging?

In the years since he'd been a young boy, he'd almost forgotten how to pray. But he prayed then, leaning against the damp wall in the stinking air of the cell. Not for strength or even release. But that his spirit, if indeed he had one, might return to Olivia after he died.

Chapter Twenty-Three

The sick feeling started in Olivia's gut as soon as Benton failed to come home with the morning light, such as it was, for it rained hard outside. Misapprehension had haunted her most the night, and she'd had little sleep. The dread increased when she ventured outside, only to encounter other residents of the building.

Many of the rooms in the squat structure were held by Lightmen. Now their wives, or as in her case, lovers, filtered out, all with the same questions on their lips and the same fear in their eyes.

"Has anyone seen my Freddie?"

"My man's very late comin' home."

"Where is he? Why isn't he back yet?"

Olivia herself did not have long before she must report to work. She walked to the tavern in hopes of finding Danny, who usually had his ear to the ground and might know something.

She found him out the back door of the place, his hair mussed and his face stark, speaking to a number of other people.

"Danny, has somethin' happened?" she asked, edging in.

His gaze moved to her. "Ye haven't heard?"

She shook her head.

"They've been taken—a number of Lightmen from our branch of the resistance."

"Taken?"

"To the cells below the Palace." He hesitated. "For sentencin'."

For an instant, Danny, his companions, and the very doorway of the tavern wavered before Olivia's eyes. A great darkness rushed up inside her. She fought her way through it to say, "Not Benton?" Surely he merely lingered somewhere, hoping to help his friends?

But Danny said, "He was among them. I'm sorry."

Olivia's legs threatened to fail her. She struggled to stand.

A woman standing beside her put a rough arm around her and asked Danny, "What can we do?"

He shook his head.

"But they're our men. We have to do somethin'!"

"Attend the hearin'?" someone else suggested.

Soberly, Danny said, "I doubt there'll be a hearin'. Things have changed. Men are now executed on the streets. The fact that they've been taken in as a group suggests this—what they've done—will be considered a high crime."

"What have they done?" Olivia asked.

Danny looked at her again and once more shook his head.

A woman said, "If they were caught in the act of makin' an attack—"

"That would do it," Danny said.

"But he promised me…" Olivia broke off when she realized she spoke aloud.

Someone else repeated, "There must be somethin' we can do."

"Go to the Council Chamber if ye like. See if their names have been posted. But I'm bettin' they're not. I'm sorry," Danny added again.

The women and others gathered there began to stumble off. Danny returned to the tavern and very softly shut the door.

Thoughts crowded Olivia's mind. If she went to the Council Chamber, all the way across town, she'd be late for work. Trouble might then descend upon her head also.

But she couldn't merely go about her business, could she, knowing Benton very likely was sitting in a cell. Knowing all too well what that was like.

She began the walk through the pounding rain. Though morning had arrived, you'd barely know it, the air as dark as if doom had arrived instead.

Perhaps it had.

On her way she met with another woman from Benton's building whose husband was a Lightman. She'd forgotten her coat and her eyes were wild.

"They've been taken," said the woman whose name, so Olivia thought, was Cassie.

"Yes."

"What will I do?"

The same question that filled Olivia's heart. Life was hard and desperate. Without Benton? Impossible to face.

"They'll be sent to the mines," Cassie said.

Or worse. If they'd been apprehended in the act of attacking a mechanical—

*But he'd promised.*

It was a long walk up the hill to the Council with the palace soaring behind. When they reached the courtyard, they searched the wall where messages were pinned behind protective glass. Nothing. It was Cassie who spied a new sheet on the door.

The guards there shifted aside to let them see.

"Can ye read?" Cassie asked.

"Yes, some."

A list of names under the grim heading, *Held For Questioning*.

Eight names.

"Is his name there? Andy. Andy Lightman."

"Yes."

As was one Benny Lightman.

Olivia's legs failed her, and she sank to the sopping ground.

\*\*\*\*

"Come forth!"

The light felt blinding when the door opened, so much so that Benton still did not see the other occupants of the cell with whom he'd shared the past hours. Even though the stone corridor boasted only a single torch, it seemed overly bright after the absolute darkness.

He and Freddie stumbled out. The others of their group were being released from further cells. His heart rose on a sudden surge of hope. Would they be let go?

To be sure, not.

"Follow," barked one of the Dogs on duty. The men fell into a line with two more Dogs behind, their truncheons at the ready.

Benton did not want a blow from a truncheon. His shoulder still hurt from that he'd received last night. His head swam, and his stomach threatened to betray him. Even though it was now empty, it wanted to heave.

"Where are ye takin' us?" Andy asked, but the Dogs ignored him. Benton caught his friend's eye. Andy looked utterly terrified.

They climbed steps. Progressed along corridors. Their surroundings grew more luxurious as they went, and they passed several checkpoints where other Dogs on duty let them through.

What time was it? Would Olivia be at work by now? Did she know what had befallen him?

They stopped outside the door of a grand chamber where still another pair of Dogs admitted them. Benton could smell his own fear.

Had they crossed into the palace? The grandeur of the room they entered argued so. It had a high ceiling with carved moldings, all in creamy white, and gold trim filigreed across the walls. Behind an elaborately carved table stood a Grey Guard.

He was tall, with gray fur, grizzled a bit around his muzzle and ears. He had keen golden eyes and wore a uniform rather than the customary gray cloak. It was charcoal-colored and chased with silver trim, a lot of it. Confidence rolled from him, and with it a keen edge of danger.

He looked up sharply when the Dogs ushered the men through the door and said, "Ah. Police Dogs, you may wait outside."

The implication being that he could handle the lot of them. Benton believed it.

The Wolf eyed each man in turn. When his gaze touched upon Benton, he felt the physical impact.

Terror.

All right, he told himself. He's just a mechanical, probably with a switch buried in the fur at his crotch.

To reach for that switch would be to die.

"I am Grey Ghost," the Wolf announced. "Assistant to the Lord High."

Oh. Were they in the Lord High's vicinity?

"You are here to answer questions. This may go very badly for you, or not so badly. If you answer honestly, you may be sent to the mines. If you do not answer honestly, it will be the Chamber." The torture chamber, he meant. "I will know whether or not you answer honestly."

He was a glorious creation, his voice box nearly flawless, producing an authoritative growl. His control was absolute, but Benton was in no position to appreciate that.

The best he could hope was for the mines. He would never see Olivia again.

The Wolf went on, "You were apprehended in the act of attacking one of the Lord High's creations, a Racoon who was at the time pursuing his legitimate business."

Legitimate? Nothing Racoons did was legal, strictly speaking. It didn't matter.

"Why did you attack him? You—" he pointed a razored claw at Freddie. "Answer me."

"Uh—" Freddie managed to croak.

Benton did not blame him for faltering, but his heart leaped in his chest. What if the Wolf picked on him next?

"Answer," the Wolf commanded.

"We—we weren't attackin' him exactly, yer reverence. We merely wanted to ask him a question."

"Lie!" the Wolf thundered. "Are you eager for the knives and irons of the Chamber?"

"No, yer reverence."

"Why did you waylay him?" the Wolf pointed at Andy.

"We wanted to see if he switched off like the Cats

and Dogs."

Benton groaned inwardly.

"Ah." The Wolf's eyes gleamed. "Are you then members of the squad who have been attacking Cats and shutting them down? Those, perhaps, who threw two Dogs into the river?"

No one spoke.

"I assure you," Grey Ghost said, "you will speak the truth one way or another. You will shout it."

A lanky man called Donnie said, "We wanted to see if we could shut them down, yes, as a peaceful solution, sir, to our misery. Now can I go home to my wife?"

The Wolf smiled. How it could be recognized as a smile, Benton could not say, as the mechanical's jaws already gaped. But a smile of sorts it seemed.

"So you have formed squads of men going about the City waylaying and shutting down the Lord High's creations."

"Not to hurt them," Donnie said, "or harm them in any way."

"Except the ones thrown into the river."

"—except the ones thrown into the river, yer reverence."

"Was this an act of defiance?" Grey Ghost pressed. "Protest?"

"Perhaps," Donnie whispered.

"You understand that the punishment for such defiance is immediate Removal? You may consider yourselves fortunate you are standing here and not already dead."

Yet. Oh, surely no, he would never see Olivia again. For an instant Benton longed for her—the scent of her, the feel of her warmth—so much it nearly overwhelmed his staggering fear.

"Which begs the question," the Wolf growled, "how did you or any men know to search out the location of a—as you call it—kill switch?"

Yes, there was the question, the one truly dangerous to someone other than themselves. To answer it would put Gloria in immediate peril. Gloria, whom they all respected and, so Benton would say, who was to be protected.

No one spoke. Grey Ghost gazed at them with patient expectation. He truly was a marvel of engineering.

"Come, now," he growled after the silence drew out. "You will tell me. Easy or hard."

The men shifted on their feet. None there doubted the nature of the hard.

Would any crack?

It seemed not right away. The shabby crew buttoned their lips and not a word escaped them.

They might not crack here before this admittedly terrifying creature. But under torture?

They were but men, after all.

Chapter Twenty-Four

Olivia took a scolding from the House Mouse when she reached her first assignment of the day after her start time. She apologized profusely and promised she would make it up, though she could not imagine how.

She could not imagine getting through the day.

She scrubbed her way through it, barely noticing for once the provision of mud, worse than usual due to the intense rain.

The very world wept for her loss.

She barely noticed her employers hissing or growling or whinnying at her, either. At the end of the day, she hurried home praying for a miracle. That Benton would be there after all. Telling her it had all been a mistake.

He was not there. The dismal little room lay cold and empty. Olivia did not stay but hurried back out and to her former room, to consult with Gloria.

Gloria was not there either. Broadsheets still littered the room, but the unmade bed was cold and Gloria's few possessions were gone.

Maybe she was still at Danny's. Or someone else had come and collected her. To hide her, perhaps.

She went next to the tavern, looking for Danny who, frustratingly, was not there.

"He's off with Madam Gloria," whispered Lenny Barman, so Olivia could barely hear. "No one knows where."

Well, yes, that made sense. Danny had demonstrated obvious feelings for Gloria. Could he keep her safe? If the members of the resistance talked—

She had a sudden blinding image of Benton under torture. Stripped down, strapped to a table, subject to unbearable agony.

What could she do to help him? To free him? Nothing. She was helpless as a newborn.

Suddenly she understood Gloria's impulse to turn herself over to the authorities. To make the sacrifice that would spare others.

Maybe Danny had taken Gloria away precisely to keep her from doing that. And likely it was too late anyway. Benton and the other members of the resistance lay already in the Lord High's hands.

What could save them?

****

Pain. A great, roaring, flaming blaze of it. Benton knew nothing more. At times it retreated to a dull agony, before they stepped up and worked on him again, asking their questions. Relentless.

He'd never imagined such a level of pain could exist. He'd thought it bad when they'd strapped him, naked, to the table, his injured shoulder pulled excruciatingly tight.

He'd swiftly learned that was nothing. He'd tried to vomit twice. There was nothing inside him to come up.

He could hear the screams of the others around him. Four stations there were in this chamber—four tables, each with a man strapped to it. Their torturers were great man-sized hairless Moles, seeming at home here underground. Benton did not know if they could see, but their aim was flawless.

Their aim with the heated irons.

He did not think anyone had crumbled. Yet. He had not heard Gloria's name spoken and he had not uttered it. Not but he'd been distracted from the others by his own agony. He'd passed out for moments at a time. But if anyone had spoken her name, why would the Moles keep up the torture?

It was only a matter of time before someone spoke. The next time they laid the iron to his scrotum, he likely would.

He would never have children now. Never be able to give Olivia a babe.

"I am impressed," growled Grey Ghost, who orchestrated the questioning, moving between the four tables and growling the questions. "I did not think you would hold out so long."

"A little more for our friend, Freddie," he said to one of the Moles. Freddie screamed. He choked words in reply to the Wolf's question.

"Where did you get your information?"

"It was on the street! On the street! We just wanted to see—"

Such courage! Benton's heart leaped in his chest. Was there hope of protecting Gloria? No hope left for them.

"The Cats being shut off were lured." Grey Ghost said with mechanical calm. "Who lured them?"

He must have given a nod. A red-hot bar came down, sizzling, onto Benton's stomach. His mind exploded, knowing only pain, and his mind flickered in and out.

*Just let me go. Please.* Death would be better than

this.

"You can make the pain stop." Grey Ghost said calmly. "You will be taken back to your cell."

Suddenly the reeking black cell seemed the finest place of refuge.

"Only tell me who planned the attacks."

"We did," he ground out. *There's your answer, bastard Wolf.* "We planned it."

"I do not think so."

Another nod. A fresh poker touched Benton's balls which had already tried to crawl up into his belly.

He winked out.

\*\*\*\*

The meeting was a wild one, completely without any semblance of order. They came together behind the weaver's shop. Danny was not there. Nor was Gloria. The rest of them wept and screeched at each other.

All to no avail. Their dear ones were lost to them, and nobody had any answers.

Mad, desperate suggestions were made. Plans for deceiving the authorities put forward. A fake trail might be laid for them to pursue. One woman even volunteered to turn herself in, planning to say she had directed the men to the attacks.

"What good will that do?" asked another. "Our men won't be freed either way. They'll be sent to the mines. We'll never see them again."

The words reinforced Olivia's own fears. She had lived that day through arguing to herself that she could—somehow—save Benton. That against all odds and likelihoods she would see him again. She went home from the meeting with her hopes dashed, terrifyingly alone.

The streets were nearly empty of people, carriages, or mechanicals. The rain rattled like steel on the cobbles, echoing. She went to Benton's room rather than her own, thinking if a miracle did occur, he would return there.

No miracles occurred. She curled into a ball in his bed, seeking the scent of him. Never had she felt so forsaken.

In the morning, early before the sun had heaved itself up above the rain clouds, someone pounded on her door. Her heart leaped, thinking it might be Benton, or news of him. But when she hauled the door open, she found only the girl from down the hall, whose husband was also a Lightman.

Rosie was her name.

"Come," Rosie said. "Danny's back and he's called a meetin'."

"Where?"

"At the tavern."

They went together, moving through the dark streets where many of the lamps remained unlit. Apparently sufficient relief Lightmen had not been found.

The room over the tavern overflowed with grim individuals. Olivia and Rosie slipped in among them, silent.

Olivia might not have recognized Danny Barman. Gone was the confident, slightly cheeky young man he had been, with the ready smile and charming patter. This man looked pale and shaken, a mere ghost of who he'd been.

He waited till the room was as full as it could be before he said, "She's gone. Gloria. Gave me the slip last night she did, when I fell asleep. Crept off without makin' a sound."

His lips trembled and tears came to his eyes. He fought them back valiantly. "Before that, she'd been talkin' about turnin' herself in, makin' a bargain with the Lord High—as if any among us has a hope of dealin' with him. He owns us all in debt, if no other way. But I'm afraid—" He paused abruptly before concluding, "I'm afraid that's where she's gone."

A terrible silence gripped the room, made up of several components. They all admired and respected Gloria. They would have protected her if they could. By the same token, did this present any hope for their men?

"How might Madam Gloria do a deal?" one woman asked. "If she goes anywhere near the palace, won't she be seized?"

"I would think so," said Danny, sounding defeated. "I can't imagine what she has in mind. I regret—I regret I was not strong enough or smart enough to prevent her takin' this course."

"Ye're human, man," said one of his fellow Barmen. "We need sleep, and ye certainly did not mean to fail her."

"I did not. I would have given my life." Danny said it plainly. Not one of them there doubted him.

"What will happen now?" asked Rosie. "Is there any hope for our men?"

Danny replied, "I can't say. I thought ye should all be advised. Her courage—" He could say no more.

Olivia thought of Gloria, frail and battered, and seared by what she'd already endured, yet a lioness inside. Would she ever possess such courage?

"I'm goin' to the Palace to wait," said Rosie. "In case my Jordie comes out."

"I'll go with ye," Olivia said, thinking of her own

release from the cells, the endless walk back up to rejoin the world, emerging into the rainy light that had seemed so bright.

Life, or so it seemed, was all relative. As humans, their world might not offer them much. But there were moments when what they did possess became very precious.

"Do not draw attention to yourselves," Danny advised. "We don't need any more prisoners taken."

Everyone there nodded somberly. The meeting dissolved and they went out into the eternal rain. Olivia barely noticed it. Her heart remained with Benton, wherever he might be.

\*\*\*\*

"On your feet."

The command seemed to come from a great distance, and Benton had no hope of obeying it. How could he stand? Surely he was still strapped to the table in the stone chamber.

The pain, still with him, had faded a titch in intensity. When he moved, seeking to test his bonds, which as he discovered no longer existed, it flared. On his chest, his stomach, all down both arms and legs. Between his legs.

He lay in the dark. Back in the cell? Had the torture ended?

He was not alone. Others around him groaned, voicing his own misery. He could not tell their groans from his own.

"On your feet, I say." The order was repeated in a growl that told Benton it came from the throat of a Dog. One of the guards, most likely.

A light flared, causing more pain, this time to

Benton's eyes. So long had he been in the dark, the brilliance hurt, and he had to blink furiously. He sought to take stock of himself.

He lay on the damp stone floor of a cell. The place was perhaps eight paces by six in size and held others of the group with whom he'd been arrested. He was naked—all of them were—and looking at his body made the sickness rise.

Was this his body? It couldn't be.

"Cover yourselves!" The Dog, who stood blocking the doorway, tossed garments at them. Someone whimpered. Benton realized it might be him.

He sat up and nearly swooned from the pain. All around him men cried out and retched.

"Move," growled the Dog, "unless you want more of the irons."

*No.* Benton could not progress beyond that thought. *No.* he struggled up, trembling.

"Please," one of the men moaned. Had he not learned better than to ask for mercy? There was none.

Benton clutched the garment that had been tossed at him and staggered. His legs did not want to hold him, and he did not know how he might force clothing over the mess that was his skin.

If it meant avoiding the irons—

The men struggled into the clothing, loose-fitting trousers and shirts, only Benton's, being too small for his large frame, did not fit and scraped on the abused skin.

"Come," said the Dog.

They were being taken from the cell. Freed? Other Dogs waited in the corridor and fell in behind their group, armed with truncheons. No one in the ragged line tried to break away.

They walked. The word did not begin to convey the agony of it. One man sobbed. Benton's mind raged and beat against the prison of his skull before settling to the task of putting one foot in front of the other.

They walked far.

Up steps that tripped them. Benton went down to one knee more than once and others fell. The Dogs pushed them up roughly.

The stone walls acquired plaster as they climbed, and then rich hangings. Carpet underfoot. Were they in the palace itself?

Someone stepped out ahead of their little train. Grey Ghost it was, clad in a fine, embroidered cloak.

At the sight of him, men cried out involuntarily.

"You will be silent!" Grey Ghost ordered. "You will not utter a sound unless you are addressed directly, under penalty of death."

Benton grunted under his breath. There were far worse penalties than death—this he knew.

"You are about to be in the presence of greatness."

Greatness? Surely Grey Ghost did not mean—

A set of double doors ahead of them swung open. Covered in gold leaf they were, and Benton's abused brain produced a crazy thought: was that what all their debt purchased? That beneath which they labored so hard, owing, owing forever. To put gilt on a palace door.

Then he had no time to think. The Dogs ushered them in.

The chamber was large, with vast walls and a soaring ceiling, and must once have been grand. Now it was cluttered with tables and benches on each side. Gears and other metal components littered every surface and the air smelled of oil and steam.

A workshop, Benton's mind told him. Here in the palace.

His thoughts were not operating properly. But they did tell him this place, this vast workroom, could belong to only one man.

The Lord High himself.

Chapter Twenty-Five

The man, tall and thin with a wild mop of gray-white hair, did not appear well. He wore a cobbler's apron like any common workman, over a set of trousers and a shirt not unlike the one Benton had been forced to don. A pair of ancient boots.

Not a young man, as the whitened hair and the lines in his face denoted. Many deep lines in his face. Humans no longer reached a great age. He must have lived through the Great Killing and all the ensuing years.

His narrow form had become permanently stooped as it might be from bending endlessly over the worktables. He had to half peer through his shaggy eyebrows at the men who were prodded into the room.

His eyes—

Oh, his eyes. They were dark, at variance with his otherwise pale aspect. Bright. Intelligent, terrifyingly so.

"Ah," he said to Grey Ghost in a cracked tremor. "Is this them? Those who seek to defy me?"

"Yes, my Lord High," Grey Ghost boomed.

The Lord High. It could be no one else. But why would they, a lowly group of humans, be brought here before him?

The men among whom Benton stood stared and trembled. One fell to his knees. "Please. Let me go. I have a wife and child. Do not send me to the mines."

"Get him up," the Lord High snapped.

Grey Ghost half hauled the man to his feet. Gave him a blow across the cheek that left furrows not unlike Benton's own.

"Did I not tell you to remain silent?"

The man sobbed quietly into his hands.

"So," the Lord High spoke to the resultant near-silence, letting that dark gaze play over them, "this is what mankind has come to. Pitiful."

It was. They were. But what chance had they been given?

"I almost feel sorry for ye. Almost," the Lord High went on, "but I lost the capacity for pity long ago. I am, however, impressed that none of ye gave up the name of your leader under torture. I shall have to invent crueler tortures, eh, Grey Ghost? More painful ones."

*Impossible*, Benton's mind screamed.

"Something to loosen tongues. It would perhaps be more painful for these men to watch their loved ones tortured than to endure the agony themselves."

*No*, Benton screamed inwardly.

The Lord High looked at the sobbing man. "Ye have a wife, ye say? A child? How would they fare beneath the irons, d'ye suppose?"

"No!" The man raised his face from his hands. "Take me back in, instead."

"Ah, such nobility! Such nobility in specimens fallen so low. Still, if ye have loved ones, ye be wealthy men despite your debts, eh?" He muttered half under his breath, "Something I never had."

So, was this what lack of love did to a person? And was Benton meant to feel bad for him?

The Lord High raised his voice a little. "Ye will be wondering why ye were brought here. I wanted to see the ilk of the men who make up a resistance. Who dare to move against me. Who have had the temerity to harm my creations! I vowed long ago to defend all I made against what made me. I must say, ye appear disappointingly ordinary."

The dark gaze fixed on Benton. "Step forward."

Benton's stomach fell and his heart rattled in his chest, but he stepped up from the others.

The Lord High raked him with a look. "What is your name?"

"Benton Lightman."

"It is Benny Lightman on the list of miscreants."

"Benny."

"How did ye acquire that wound on your face, Benny?"

Benton had a sudden vision of Olivia tending the gouges, dabbing gently with concern in her eyes. His heart swelled with love.

"On the street, Lord High. From a Grey Guard."

"Ah. An honest man. This was acquired in the course of trying to shut down my creation?"

"Yes, Lord High."

"Who told ye where the kill switches are located?"

A trap. He had not answered that question under torture. He would not do so now.

"It was a rumor heard on the street, Lord High. We wanted to see if it was true. It was."

"A rumor."

"Yes, Lord High. Passed from lip to lip."

"But ye do not know where this rumor originated."

"No, Lord High."

The man in the cobbler's apron eyed Benton. "Ye are meant for the mines. Ye, particularly, will make a fine workman, given yer size. We always need men in the mines, since our world runs on coal, and unfortunately men do not survive long in that environment. No man ever returns from the mines. But we get the worth of their feed out of them before they expire."

Benton swayed on his feet, feeling Olivia slip away from him. Never to see her again. Never to hold her again.

"However," the Lord High went on, "ye are not to be sent to the mines. Yer freedom has been bought."

What? Bought? Who—

"Bring her in," ordered the Lord High.

Grey Ghost nodded obediently. He signaled to the Dog that guarded not the outer door but a narrow aperture at the rear of the cluttered room.

The group of men waited. A shuffling sounded and three figures entered through the rear door.

She looked impossibly small trapped between the two Dogs, one a Labrador and the other an Alsatian. They towered over her frail form, the thin limbs, the patchy hair still only partly grown in. Her eyes, dark like those of the Lord High, shot them all a brilliant look before dropping to the floor.

No, Benton thought incoherently. Oh, no. They had suffered so much to protect her. And here she was.

Her hands—scarred by tortures with which Benton was now intimately familiar—were bound in front of her. She wore a ragged coat still wet from the rain and looked otherwise unharmed.

The Lord High threw back his head, not an easy task, given his severe stoop. "Do ye know this woman?"

No one answered. The men all appeared stricken.

Gloria raised her eyes. "Do not lie," she said in a surprisingly strong voice. "He knows the truth, that it was I who told ye how to find the kill switches. I—who betrayed him."

"He betrayed us," cried a man in the back, bravely. "His own kind, for a bunch of mechanicals."

It took courage to speak out, but they all adored Gloria, these men. She had given them hope when nothing existed except mud, and debt. And rain, like continual tears.

Anyway, their courage was nothing compared to hers. She had turned herself over knowing what lay in store for her.

"I have bought your freedom," Gloria said. "I have done so out of love. Go home to your families. Do not misbehave again, for in the future I will not be able to save ye."

Disconcertingly, terrifyingly, two tears ran down her face. She looked so utterly vulnerable standing there between the old man and the Dogs, Benton's heart clamored in protest. The men around him muttered.

"Live your lives," Gloria told them, "for those ye love."

"But we love ye," Freddie choked out, the burns on his body testifying to the truth of it.

"I have betrayed the Lord High and must pay the price."

"Enough of all this," cried the Lord High, his face twisted with distaste. "I despise such maudlin claptrap. Take her away."

The men stirred, protest arriving among them in one surge. The Dogs and Gray Ghost stepped forward, the Dogs raising their truncheons. Before anyone could act,

Gloria had been escorted back through the rear door.

Gone.

Benton did not imagine she would ever see the light of day again.

"What good is it to punish her now?" asked Freddie, still fired up. "We already know your great secret and can shut down your powerful creations any time we like."

It was a bold statement, if a foolish one.

The Lord High focused on Freddie. For an instant Benton almost heard words of condemnation from the old man's lips—for Freddie and for all of them. They would be taken back to the torture room where he would surely die.

But the Lord High said, "If ye think I will leave the kill switches located where they are, ye are very much mistaken. Modifications will be implemented."

But he was one man, one set of hands. That would take time.

"Your freedom has been purchased. I am a man of my word," he repeated. "One time—for this one offense. If I see any of ye here again, it will be the mines."

He said to Grey Ghost, "Release them. But keep a careful eye."

"Yes, Lord High."

They left the chamber, exiting through the main doors as they had come in. Benton stumbled a bit over his own feet in his eagerness to get away, and yet his heart ached.

Ached for the tiny woman they left behind.

What would the Lord High do to her? What punishment might he devise?

A new thought struck him: their suffering to protect

her meant nothing, since she had turned herself over anyway.

And yes, she would pay a heavy price.

In a wretched, suffering crowd they traversed a broad corridor, passed through a large outer chamber where people and mechanicals, most of them Cats, stared. A wide pair of doors, open to the daylight, beckoned from beyond.

Freedom.

They broke into a fast walk at the end, some of them helping the others. At the doors, Grey Ghost spoke to the Dogs on guard, who stepped aside.

They went out of the Council Chambers and into the rain.

And it felt wonderful even though it hurt. Cold and somehow cleansing, as if it might wash their pain away. It could not. There would be a long period of healing. Benton's shoulder, in particular, would need time to heal, if it ever did.

But he was out in the world. *Free*.

There seemed to be a lot of people collected in the plaza in front of the building, ragged humans staring at them through the rain. They began to exclaim. Some screamed and ran forward. Cries of disbelief and delight.

Benton saw Olivia there among them.

What was she doing here? He wondered in confusion. She should be at work. She would get in trouble.

His legs wavered beneath him and threatened to fail. Olivia flew to him and barreled into his arms, and then she was holding him up. Crying his name.

*Benton, Benton, Benton.*

"I am Benton." A man. One not to be demeaned with

a diminutive name, but one who had withstood torture. A man of dignity.

"We've been freed," he told her. "Gloria—she turned herself in. Sacrificed herself."

"We know."

Olivia kissed him, and for that one moment nothing else existed—not the rain or the debt or the fear or the wounds upon his tortured skin, but only the love she offered him and he accepted.

Was life truly so simple as that? Was it all about the love? And might that be mankind's greatest weapon?

"Come." Olivia was sobbing when the kiss ended. She touched his hands, his arms, his face, grief flooding her eyes at what she beheld. "I am so glad, so very glad to see ye. Let us go home."

They went, Benton still stumbling, and Olivia with her arm wrapped around him. They turned their backs to the horror behind them and moved through the rain and over the mud to a future unknown.

Epilog

Olivia stood against the rough boards of the wall and eyed the motley group gathered in the room above the tavern. The meeting had been going on for hours, people shouting and having their say, and looked to continue for a while yet.

In days gone by, she might have chosen this position because it afforded a quick escape. Now her heart was anchored here to these people and to one man in particular.

She would never leave him. Not till she died.

Her gaze found him where he sat, for he still found it difficult to remain on his feet for any length of time. What he'd suffered at the hands of the Lord High's torturers had been debilitating. She'd done what she could for him and had even called in a physician, one who had mercifully treated the tortured men free of charge, thereby not sending Olivia deeper into debt. But his scarred body told a tale, and his shoulder might never be right. He'd been forced to resume his job at once. Somehow, he'd endured.

No matter, she told herself firmly, letting the heated words spoken in the room wash over her, for she still had him. He slept in her arms when she returned from her own labors, before he had to begin his, and on Sundays. He still—quite miraculously, considering what had been done to him—was able to love her.

As if he felt her gaze upon him, Benton raised his eyes to hers. Light flared there—no longer plain mud-colored to her, those eyes, but lit with green and amber. With love and courage.

A promise lay in his eyes. This man kept his promises.

"We must do all we can to rescue her," Danny Barman thundered. He had become quite a firebrand since Gloria's return to captivity. Without question, he was their leader now that the woman he loved had disappeared back into obscurity.

No doubt at all that this man, who had sought to make love to so many, now loved but one alone.

His hearers nodded soberly. An act of courage it was, even to continue meeting this way, to keep the resistance alive. A heartbeat against the darkness.

But as those who met seemed to agree tacitly, if the resistance died, so would the last of their hope.

Gloria had become a martyr and a cause even though they did not know if she was alive or dead.

Danny continued speaking with passion. Yes, the Lord High had forged ahead with modifications to his creations, beginning, it was said, with the Cats and moving on to the Grey Guard. but he had only one set of hands. Those modifications were many. They, the resistors, still had time to lure and waylay more Cats, whose numbers were already down. If they had the courage.

Courage, and love. Both vital requirements, it seemed.

"But the Cats are on to us," someone objected. "They'll no longer be lured by false reports of mice or rats."

265

"False?" Danny smiled and signaled to a girl by the door. "Bring 'em in."

The girl pressed into the adjacent storeroom and slipped back in with a box in her hands. Even from Olivia's post at the wall, she could see the box held a scrap of blanket. As for what else it held—

Gasps told that the people in the front of the room had got a look. Benton levered himself up from his bench and then shot Olivia an incredulous glance, motioning her forward.

Everyone pressed up and held their breath.

The box contained living creatures. Five of them. Not mechanicals. Not even miniature mechanicals meant to fit in a box. But living beings. A miracle.

"Where—" someone gasped.

"On the docks where I work," the girl, Lizzie, said. "I heard them. Their mother was dead and a few others of the babies. I took these—" She hesitated. "Aren't they cute?"

They were. Olivia did not remember ever having seen baby animals—living animals—just pictures. These were incredibly small, with new downy hair growing in over their bodies.

Tiny, baby mice.

"Lizzie has been raisin' them, feedin' them," Danny said. "But I'm sure the point will not have been lost on any of ye.

"We need not lure the Cats with rumors or stories. What could attract them better than the knowledge of actual mice returned to the City?"

A brief, awed silence reigned before someone said, "But we can't let the Cats hurt them."

"No," Lizzie gasped.

No. The mice were a miracle, pure and simple.

"Don't worry," Danny said. "We'll be there to protect them."

Olivia exchanged a look of wonder with Benton before she returned her gaze to the tiny, squirmy creatures.

Courage, love, and miracles, she thought. Seemed a much stronger combination than mere mud, debt, and gears.

## A word about the author...

Multi-award-winning author Laura Strickland delights in time traveling to the past and searching out settings for her books, be they Historical Romance, Steampunk or something in between. Venturing beyond Historical and Contemporary Romance, she created a new world with her ground-breaking Buffalo Steampunk Adventure series set in her native city, in Western New York.

Married and the parent of one grown daughter, Laura has also been privileged to mother a number of very special rescue dogs, and is intensely interested in animal welfare. Her love of dogs, and her lifelong interest in Celtic history, magic and music, are all reflected in her writing.

Laura's mantra is Lore, Legend, Love, and she wouldn't have it any other way.